"The students deserve a clean, safe place for their learning… Don't you agree, Levi?"

His head was spinning over all the words she managed to get out in a few seconds. He started to answer her, but she began talking again.

"As soon as the paint dries, we can get the shades back up on the windows and then I can start hauling in the boxes of books. I'm excited, Levi, because it's looking like we'll be done on time."

"*Ja.* That it does. You're a good worker."

He didn't know why he said those words to her. She was a "good worker." That sounded so impersonal, like he was speaking to one of the male helpers. But his compliment brought a light blush to her cheekbones and Levi found himself wanting to smile.

"*Danke.* I just want everything to be perfect for the students."

"With your enthusiasm, I'm certain that it will be."

Mesmerized by the sparkle of hope reflected in her blue eyes, Levi found it hard to look away from Sadie.

An Amazon top ten bestselling historical romance author, **Tracey J. Lyons** was a 2017 National Excellence in Romance Fiction Award finalist. She sold her first book on 9/9/99! A true Upstate New Yorker, Tracey believes you should write what you know. Tracey considers herself a small-town gal who writes small-town romances. Visit www.traceyjlyons.com to learn more about her.

Books by Tracey J. Lyons

Love Inspired

A Love for Lizzie
The Amish Teacher's Wish

Visit the Author Profile page at Harlequin.com.

The Amish Teacher's Wish

Tracey J. Lyons

ISBN-13: 978-1-335-55426-0

The Amish Teacher's Wish

This edition published by arrangement with Harlequin Books S.A.

For questions and comments about the quality of this book, please contact us at CustomerService@Harlequin.com.

Love Inspired
22 Adelaide St. West, 40th Floor
Toronto, Ontario M5H 4E3, Canada
www.Harlequin.com

Printed in U.S.A.

But I will hope continually,
and will yet praise thee more and more.
—*Psalms* 71:14

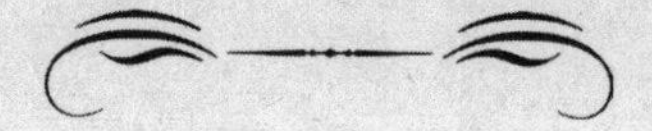

This book is dedicated
to the loving memory of my dad;
Theodore J. Pinkowski—gone but never forgotten.
Cheers, Dad!

Chapter One

Miller's Crossing
Chautauqua County, New York

Sadie Fischer should have known better. After the rains they'd had this past week, the hillsides were muddy. She probably should have stayed on the main road. But, *nee*, she was in a hurry to see her friend Lizzie Burkholder and to deliver the latest supply of quilted pot holders she had made for the store Lizzie ran with her husband, Paul. A schoolteacher here in Miller's Crossing, Sadie helped her *mamm* with small quilting projects during the summer months when school was not in session.

As she hurried along the old cow path shortcut through the field at the bottom of the hill below the *Englischer*'s church, Sadie was glad her students couldn't see their teacher now. It hadn't taken long for her haste to catch up with her. A few steps onto the path, and her feet started sinking into the soggy earth. She always chided her students for trying to take shortcuts in their schoolwork. She couldn't help but smile, thinking how they'd be the ones wagging their fingers at her now.

Looking down, she grimaced. Her feet were almost ankle-deep in the murky water. The soles of her shoes were caked with mud. Her *mamm* would have her doing the dishes for months if she caught her in this predicament. Oh, Sadie could almost hear her *mamm* scolding her now, reminding Sadie to pay attention to where she was going.

Of all her siblings, Sadie was the most talkative and the most distracted. In her *mamm*'s words, she was a *blabbermaul*. She couldn't help being chatty. As the youngest, she'd learned at an early age to speak up in order to be heard over the din of her sisters and brothers. She had three of each. When the others were busy with chores, she'd also learned how to fend for herself and to take shortcuts.

Clinging tightly to the bag filled with the pot holders, Sadie attempted to lift one leg and then the other out of the sloppy mess.

She hoped she could make her way out of this quagmire and back to the main road.

"Oh, dear," she murmured, looking down to where the mud now bubbled around her feet. Her movements only caused her to sink farther into the soft ground.

Blowing out a breath, she looked around for something to grab hold of. Spotting a low-hanging tree branch a few feet away, she thought she might be able to grab hold of that and pull herself out. Although, she'd need to find a safe place to put her bag. Lifting her arm, she flung the bag high into the air, watching it land on a dry spot in the field a few feet away from the cow path.

Next, she stretched her right arm as far as she could for the branch, her muscles straining against the effort. The leaves tickled her fingers, and her heartbeat kicked up. She was so close to getting out of this mess. She had the first bit of the branch in her hand when suddenly it snapped free, sending her backward. Sadie let out a yelp as she fell with a splash into the mud.

"Nee! Nee!"

She sat there looking down at her blue dress now covered in mud, the cool wetness seeping through the fabric. A honeybee buzzed around her head. Without thinking, she swatted at it, splashing more mud up onto her prayer *kapp*. She wanted to cry. But crying wasn't in her nature. However, getting out of the many messes she always seemed to end up in was.

Once again, she looked around for something she could grab hold of to pull herself out of this muck. When she couldn't find anything, it seemed like the only thing to do might be to give up what remained of her pride and crawl out onto the drier part of the field. She made a face at the idea of getting even dirtier. Still, she was just about to give it a try when she heard the sound of a wagon.

Craning her neck, she spotted a long work wagon coming up over the rise in front of the church.

She waved her arms in the air and shouted, "Help! Help!"

At first, she wasn't sure the driver could hear her, so she yelled louder. "Help! I need help!"

She sent up a prayer of thanksgiving as the wagon pulled to a stop in the church parking lot. A man jumped down from the wagon. He was too far away for her to tell if she knew him. He stood with a hand shielding his eyes from the sunlight, looking out over the field. Maybe he couldn't see her.

Sadie waved her arms over her head, hoping to catch his attention. "I'm over here! Over here!"

She breathed a sigh of relief when he began to run toward her. By the time he got to her, she had only managed to dig herself even deeper into the mud. That's what she got for trying to get up on her own.

"Miss, are you all right?"

"*Ja.* I'm just stuck in this mud pit." She tried to laugh but couldn't quite manage it.

"That you are. Here, let me help you up."

When he moved closer, Sadie realized she'd never seen him before. The depth of his hazel-colored eyes struck her—hues of blues, greens and browns all mixed together. His fine cheekbones were cut high on his face, and his hair was a touch lighter brown than most of the men's around here. She also noticed he wore his suspenders fastened on the outside and not on the inside of his pants like the men in her community.

A million questions flew through her mind. Where had he come from? Why was he here? Was he just passing through Miller's Crossing? And if so, where was he headed?

He raised an eyebrow, his mouth pressing into a thin line. "Miss, I don't have all day to stand here while you make up your mind about staying or letting me help you out of your predicament."

Surprised by the abruptness in his voice, Sadie replied in her best schoolteacher voice, "There's no need to use that tone with me."

He drew back his shoulders. *"Es dutt mir leed."*

Sadie narrowed her eyes, wondering if his apology was sincere. His gaze softened a bit. "I accept your apology."

The wetness was seeping into her skin, and she looked down at the mess she'd made of herself. When she looked back up, she found the stranger extending his hand to her.

She hesitated, then took hold of it, surprised as his large hand swallowed hers in a firm grip. She let out a yelp as he tugged her up to stand beside him on the dry grass.

Sadie felt his warmth against her side and took an acceptable step backward. It wouldn't be proper for her to be seen out in a field, alone, with any man, especially with someone she didn't even know. She imagined the scolding she'd get from the elders who ran the school if they could see her now. No doubt not unlike the one she would get from her *mamm* when she saw the mess Sadie had made.

Due to her reputation within the community for being, what some would consider, too outgoing, Sadie had struggled to convince the board to let her teach the students in the first place. With no one else available for the last year, they'd reluctantly agreed to let her take over on a temporary basis. But with summer and harvest time nearing an end and still no permanent teacher found, Sadie had been given another chance to prepare for the upcoming semester.

She hadn't seen teaching as a lifelong endeavor, more as something to hold her over until she met the man who would become her husband. However, while all her friends had married off to eligible men in Miller's Crossing, Sadie had been left with suitors who were either too old or too young. So, for now, she was content to focus on *her* students. Though she knew it was wrong to think of them as hers, it was hard not to feel that way when she had no husband or *kinder* of her own yet.

Although if her parents had their way, Sadie would be forced into a courtship with Isaiah Troyer. The man was older than her, a widower with no children. She had no desire to be involved with him even if her *vader* thought they could be a *gut* match.

She knew the right man was out there. She just had to be patient in finding him.

Pushing those thoughts aside, she rubbed her hands together and thanked the tall, lanky man at her side. "*Danke.* If not for you, I might have had to crawl my way out."

His eyes took on a deeper brown hue as he folded his arms across his chest and looked down at her. "Then it's a *gut* thing for you I came along when I did."

"*Ja.*"

"I've got to be in town for an appointment. I can drop you someplace if you'd like." He studied her for a moment. When she hesitated, he shrugged and turned away.

"*Ja*, a ride would be nice. If you wouldn't mind," Sadie said. Hurrying to pick up the bag of pot holders, she followed him.

Halfway to the wagon, he paused so she could catch up. "Dare I ask why you were stuck in the mud?"

She blinked up at him. "I…um… I was taking a shortcut to my friend's house. And as you can see, that didn't end well."

"Am I taking you there?"

Sadie knew she needed to change out of

her wet clothes before she did anything else. The pot holders would have to wait. "*Nee.* You can take me home."

They walked the rest of the way to the wagon in silence. Pausing alongside it, she put her hand on the seat to hoist herself up.

"Do you need help getting up?"

"*Nee.* I can do it," she assured him.

But when she put her wet foot up on the step, it slipped off, throwing her backward. If not for the grace of God, she might have landed on her backside again. She managed to right herself just in time.

The stranger rushed to her side, but Sadie waved him off. While she may have needed help getting out of the mudhole, she could handle getting into a wagon on her own.

"I'm fine."

Nodding, he walked around to the other side of the wagon and climbed up.

Sadie scraped her shoe across the dirt in the parking lot to give the sole a little grit, then managed to get up onto the seat without any more mishaps. Settling a respectable distance away from him, she pulled her skirt in close, hoping to keep the seat free from the mud.

Blowing out a breath, she looked over the

vista spreading out below the church. The view always filled her with hope and happiness. In her mind, this was the prettiest place in all of Miller's Crossing, even all of Chautauqua County, New York. Her family's Amish community had settled here back in the middle of the last century. Her ancestors had come from Ohio, leaving scarce farmland to make a living here.

Sadie wiggled around on the seat, trying to ignore the fact that the mud was beginning to dry. She looked down at the floorboard where drips of mud were falling off her shoes.

"I'm afraid I'm making a mess of your wagon."

The man didn't respond. He nudged the single workhorse along with a flick of the leather reins. He appeared to be focused on the roadway and not her. Only now did she notice the way his eyes were narrowed as if he were in deep concentration, and there were grim lines around his mouth.

A smile could make those disappear.

"I'm Sadie Fischer."

Keeping his hand steady on the reins, he said, "I'm Levi Byler."

In all his days, Levi had never seen a young

lady looking such a sight. Mud covered most of her, and streaks of dirt ran through the loosened strands of her blond hair. A smudge of mud was drying on her chin. He had to hand it to her. Most women he knew would be crying right about now. But Miss Fischer sat there smiling at him like nothing had happened.

Her light blue eyes seemed to take in the sight of him. Levi swallowed. He knew better than to be sucked in by a woman's ostensibly innocent smile. He struggled to ignore the ache in his chest. The hurt of his recent breakup was still too fresh. On most days since that horrible time, he managed to go about his business quietly, but then there were days like today. He'd taken a wrong turn on his way to Miller's Crossing and ended up on this road.

He was coming to help his cousin Jacob Herschberger with his shed business and to heal his broken heart. Levi hoped that lending his expertise as a craftsman would not only be useful to Jacob but also aid in his own healing. He figured if he kept his hands busy, then his mind wouldn't wander to the past.

Pushing those thoughts aside, he stole a glance out of the corner of his eye at the woman sitting next to him. He supposed it was a good thing he'd come along when he did, otherwise there was no telling what would have happened to Miss Fischer.

"Where are you headed?" she asked.

Concentrating on the unfamiliar road ahead, Levi did his best to ignore the soft, friendly lilt of her voice. Her tone reminded him of the woman who'd broken his heart.

Keeping his answer simple, he replied, "I'm going to help out a family member."

"Does this person have a name? I know all of the Amish families around here."

His emotional situation was not her fault, so Levi answered, "Jacob Herschberger."

"Oh, his wife, Rachel, is a cousin to my best friend, Lizzie Burkholder. Lizzie is from the Miller family, the same ones who first settled this area. She and her husband, Paul, have a furniture and art store in Clymer," Miss Fischer went on. "Lizzie does beautiful watercolor landscapes. I wish I had half her talent. The only thing I can make are quilted pot holders from my *mamm*'s fabric scrap pile. I sell them at Lizzie's store. That's where I was heading when I got sucked into the mud."

She paused and Levi thought she might

be taking a break, but in the next breath she asked, "So, you'll be working on Jacob's sheds?"

"Ja."

"That's a *gut* thing. I know he's been looking for help. He and Rachel have a small house on the other side of the village, close to his shop. Where are you traveling from?"

Levi gave her a sideways glance, wondering if she ever stopped talking. "A district near Fort Ann," he said, keeping his answer short hoping to satisfy her curiosity.

"Oh. That's a long trip for a horse and wagon. I haven't been anyplace other than Miller's Crossing, and of course the village of Clymer."

"I came in on the bus." He didn't feel it necessary to tell her that he'd picked the horse and wagon up in the village. Levi wasn't interested in anything beyond getting her to where she needed to be in one piece.

"That was smart of you."

"Miss Fischer, you still haven't told me where you'd like to be dropped off."

"I'm afraid my *mamm* is going to be upset when she sees me looking a mess and returning home with the bag of pot holders. You can leave me at the end of my road if you'd like.

That way you won't have to hear her scolding me."

"In order for me to do that, you'll need to tell me where the end of your road is. I do need to be somewhere," he said in a soft tone, hoping to coax directions out of her.

"It's not that late in the day." She gave him a small smile. "But you are right. I'm the one troubling you, not the other way around."

He waited for a second, raised an eyebrow and asked again. "Miss Fischer, the directions to your house?"

"Ja." She pointed straight ahead. "Just over that rise, right on the other side of that cow fence, you will find my driveway."

Levi's patience was wearing thin. Perhaps it was the long trip he'd taken added to meeting this woman and wondering about his new job. With the pain of his past still fresh in his mind, he just wanted to be left alone. He didn't want to worry about Sadie Fischer. He wanted to selfishly drown in the sorrow of his heartbreak for a bit longer.

But his past had nothing to do with Sadie. She had needed help and he'd come along at the right time. He wasn't sure if he wanted to leave her alone on the road. Levi didn't feel like being friendly, but he wouldn't leave someone in distress either.

He pulled up to her drive and looked over at her. The spark seemed to have left her. Her shoulders sagged as she turned to hop down from the wagon seat.

He started to apologize, and then suddenly it wasn't her face he was seeing. *Nee*, it was the face of the woman who had shunned him.

Levi blinked. The pain of betrayal welled up inside him again. No matter how sweet Sadie Fischer appeared to be, no matter how much she might need someone to be a buffer between her and her *mamm*, he had to protect his heart. He simply could not allow himself to be drawn in again.

Over her shoulder, he saw a long tree-lined drive leading to her family's property and in the distance the roofline of a house. The better side of him—the old Levi—was starting to feel a bit of remorse for his short temper.

"Please, let me drive you the rest of the way."

Chapter Two

"*Nee.* I told you I'd be fine and I will be. I know you've someplace to be," Sadie replied as she stood on the side of the road, making a sad attempt to straighten her soggy skirts.

She paused to look up at the man. She'd kept him long enough.

"I wish you a good day, Mr. Byler," she said in a soft voice. And she meant that. Crankiness never got one anywhere in life, which is why she always tried to find the bright spot.

"*Gut* day to you," he said, giving her a courteous nod before heading on his way.

Lizzie waited for the wagon to be out of sight. She shook her head, thinking that he hadn't had such a good start to his first day in Miller's Crossing. Deciding to pay him no more attention, she turned and began to walk to the house.

She passed the complex of white barns with black trim where her *daed* had the farm equipment lined up nearby. The hay baler was missing. No doubt he was out in the field working on the recent cutting.

Sadie smiled as a small flock of white hens skittered over to her, pecking around the toes of her shoes. Seeing them reminded her she'd yet to collect today's eggs.

Letting out a sigh, she hurried along, hoping to skirt around the backside of the house and enter through the mudroom before anyone saw her. She glanced back at her muddy shoe prints. Sadie hoped her *mamm* was in a *gut* mood, otherwise she'd be in for it. Her dirty skirts slapped against her stockings as she ran behind the house.

A movement in the shadows behind the screen door caught Sadie's eye as she stepped onto the cement stoop. It appeared she wasn't going to best her *mamm* after all. The screen door flew open, slapping against the clapboard siding. A tall dark-haired woman came out onto the porch, her face flushed. Sadie sucked in a breath.

Wagging a finger at her, *Mamm*'s voice

rose. "Sadie Fischer! What mess have you gotten yourself into this time?"

"*Mamm.* I'm sorry. I tried to take the shortcut into the village and got stuck in a big mudhole down behind the *Englisch* church on Clymer Hill Road."

"And who dropped you off? I didn't recognize the wagon."

"How did you know I was dropped off?"

"I was coming in from the barn and saw you up at the top of the driveway. I'd have waited for you, but I had my hands full carrying a basket of eggs."

"I was going to gather those as soon as I cleaned up," Sadie told her.

"The day was wasting and your sister needed them for her cake mix." In a gentler voice, her *mamm* added, "You know better than to be alone with someone you don't know."

Sadie knew *Mamm* was right about that. She did her best to explain what had happened. "Levi Byler helped me out and then he kindly offered to bring me home. He's a cousin of Jacob Herschberger, so he's not really a stranger. He will be working at Jacob's shed company."

Her *mamm* gave her a sideways glance.

"You are the schoolteacher, and you are held to a higher standard in the community."

"I do understand that, *Mamm*. But if not for Levi Byler coming by when he did, I'm afraid I'd still be stuck in the mud."

"Well, then you should have brought him down here so I could have thanked him properly."

Sadie nodded. She saw no need to tell her *mamm* that the stranger had been distracted and in a hurry to be on his way.

Looking her up and down, *Mamm* scolded her again. "Sadie, today of all days, you decide to take that shortcut! And you didn't get the pot holders delivered like you promised. Furthermore, you know we have your special dinner guest coming over."

Sadie made a face. She felt bad about the pot holders but didn't care much about Isaiah. She knew he was a man of means. He had his own farm, after all. But when it came to matters of the heart, a man's stature in the community shouldn't matter. Even so, her parents were set on making this match.

Sadie thought the man would be more appropriate for her sister Sara. She'd always acted years older than her age.

"I know what you're thinking, Sadie."

Her *mamm*'s voice softened. "You think we should be more concerned with marrying off Sara. But worrying over you is what keeps your *vader* and me awake most nights. You've a way about you. And this traipsing off into the mud is yet another reason why we want you to have your future secured. You can't keep doing things on impulse."

Sadie met her *mamm*'s gaze, seeing both concern and love reflected in her eyes. She almost gave in. Sometimes she thought it might be easier to let her parents choose her spouse for her. But then she remembered that this was her life, and she was determined to live it her way. Even if it went against what her parents considered to be right. Sadie wasn't doing harm to anyone. She lived a good faithful life led by her church's teachings. She worked tirelessly to bring her beliefs into her classroom and to teach her students about acts of kindness and love.

"Think about what I've said," her *mamm* said.

The last thing Sadie wanted was to disappoint her parents, but on this one topic she would remain steadfast.

Sitting down on the stoop, she pulled off her shoes. "Yuck." She set them on the edge of the cement step. Then, standing, she rolled down her stockings and placed them with the shoes. She wiggled her toes, feeling the coolness of the air touch her skin.

"You might as well come inside the mudroom and leave your skirt here," her *mamm* said from behind her. "And anything else that has mud on it."

"Ja."

"Get inside before someone else sees you." Her *mamm* held the door open for her.

Sadie walked past her into the small coatroom off the back of the kitchen and stepped out of her skirt, now heavy with the dried mud. She unpinned her prayer *kapp* and caught her *mamm* narrowing her eyes and giving her another stern once-over. Perhaps she'd really gone too far this time.

"*Mamm*, I'm sorry for making such a mess. May I go wash up?"

She nodded. "When you are finished, you come right back to the kitchen. Your sister and I have been working to get the food ready for *your* dinner. You can wash the dishes."

Washing dishes had always been her least favorite chore. Sadie expected nothing less as her punishment. Holding her prayer *kapp* in one hand, she headed upstairs to the bathroom just past the bedroom she shared with her sister Sara. She turned on the cold water in the sink and carefully rinsed the mud off the *kapp*. Hanging it on the rack to dry, she turned her attention to peeling off the rest of her garments.

She made quick work of washing up and then went across the hall to her bedroom to change into another light blue dress and apron. Once she had pinned a fresh *kapp* on her head, Sadie took in a deep breath, blew it out and prepared to meet her *mamm* in the kitchen.

Mamm greeted her in the doorway. "Ah. Here you are, all cleaned up. *Gut*. Now let's get you to work on those dishes."

"I'll get my clothes washed up after I've done the dishes," Sadie told her *mamm*, knowing that would be her next concern. *Cleanliness is next to godliness.* The old phrase popped into her thoughts.

Walking over to the double sink, Sadie made quick work of the first batch of dishes and then listened as her *mamm* and sister discussed the upcoming meal.

"We'll make mashed potatoes to go with the roast beef," Sara said. "We want to be sure to impress Isaiah. For Sadie's sake, of course."

Sadie's head snapped up. She heard something in the tone of Sara's voice that made her think that perhaps her sister might be excited about their dinner guest.

"Sadie," her *mamm* said, "when you've finished with the dishes, you can get out the tablecloth."

The tablecloth to which her *mamm* referred was only used on very special occasions. The last time it came out of the drawer was for her *bruder* John's wedding dinner. He and his wife, Rebecca, had had a small family ceremony here on the property two years ago.

Sadie began to worry.

She didn't want to be married off to just anyone. *Ja*, like every girl she dreamed of one day falling in love, but in Amish communities, courtships and marriages weren't always about love. A lot of times *vaders* picked the match for their *dochders*.

But she didn't need to be watched over by someone older than her nineteen years. Isaiah Troyer's first wife had died soon after their marriage. She shook her head. She didn't want to be married to an older widower.

She found the tablecloth her *mamm* wanted.

Spreading it out on the table, she inhaled the delicious aromas coming from the kitchen. The roast smelled like onions and garlic. A pot of potatoes sat on the back of the stove, ready for mashing. Again, she thought all of this effort a terrible waste of everyone's precious time. But there was little to be done about this situation without causing a whole bunch of trouble.

The living room clock chimed four times. And then came the sound of a low rumble of thunder.

Her *mamm* let out a gasp and spun around from the counter where she'd been gathering the milk and butter for the potatoes. "Oh my! Sounds like there's a storm brewing."

Sadie ran to the front door and, sure enough, the sky to the north had taken on a very ominous appearance. Dark clouds swirled about. This time of year, with the high humidity and hot days, pop-up thunderstorms were common. But she had a feeling this one might turn into more than your run-of-the-mill storm. A flock of birds flew from the large oak tree in the side yard, their noise startling her. Even the hens seemed to be running for the cover of the henhouse.

"Do you see your *vader* out there?" her *mamm* asked.

Sadie looked up the drive. Trees swayed as a hard wind blew through them. Off in the distance, lightning flickered against the dark sky, followed by another roll of thunder. It looked like the strike was right near the schoolhouse. Sadie began to worry, not only for the school but for her *vader*. There was no sign of his wagon. He should be coming in from the field by now.

Relief flooded through her when she saw the barn door being rolled open and her *vader*'s form stepping outside. He struggled to push the door closed and then ran across the yard just as fat, round raindrops pelted the hard earth.

"We're in for it with this one," he said to Sadie as she held the door for him. "I saw Isaiah when I was coming in from the back field. He sends his apologies but he had to go home to his farm. He has animals outside in the pen. He needs to get them to safety. He said his knee pain was kicking up, telling him this storm could be a bad one."

Sadie held back her relief and managed to say, "*Es dutt mir leed* to hear that."

"Dochder." Her *vader* raised one of his

bushy eyebrows, giving her a knowing look. Leaning in, he whispered to her, "I'm not sure you are all that sorry."

"I'm sorry there's a bad storm coming," she said with a tiny smile.

Patting her on the shoulder, he said, "There will be another time for our special dinner."

Sadie turned her attention back to the storm. A shiver ran down her spine. The clouds blackened as the air churned. She let out a yelp when a branch broke off the maple tree in the front yard, landing on the porch steps.

"Come away from that door this instant, Sadie!" her *mamm* shouted as another crack of lightning hit close by the house.

Doing as she was told, she slammed the front door closed. And in that moment, she found herself praying that Levi Byler had safely found his way to Jacob's house.

Levi pulled into the parking area near Jacob's shed company just as the first wave of thunder rolled through Miller's Crossing. A man came running out of the large steel structure, and Levi immediately recognized his cousin.

It had been a few years since they'd seen

each other at a construction safety symposium in Saratoga Springs. At the time, Jacob had hinted that his company was growing at a fast pace, while Levi had been preparing his own future, one that included marriage.

It amazed him how quickly things had changed. One day he was happy and the next he'd found himself alone, uncertain where his life should be heading next. When Jacob had called and offered him the work, Levi's parents insisted he move to Miller's Crossing.

While Levi was happy for his cousin's success, he still wished his own future had gone the way he'd planned.

"Pull the horse and wagon into the barn over there!" Jacob shouted, pointing to the structure on the far side of the driveway.

The leather strap tugged in Levi's hands when the horse shied away from a sudden gust of wind. Carefully, he led the beast and the wagon to the safety of the barn. Jacob followed him in and rolled the barn door halfway closed behind them.

Wiping the rain from his face, Jacob said, "You've picked a fine time to arrive."

Jumping down from the wagon, Levi started to unhitch the horse. "*Ja*, this storm came up pretty fast."

"I was hoping you'd be here earlier," Jacob said. Taking the reins, he led the horse to a free stall.

"I had to stop and help out a young woman. She was stuck in the mud way down in a field behind the church at the top of the hill."

Jacob paused, looked over his shoulder at Levi and raised an eyebrow. "A young woman stuck in the mud?"

"Sadie Fischer. Do you know her? She tells me she knows you and your wife."

"We know her. That one is fiery."

Levi pondered the comment. He supposed that was one way to describe her, though *chatty* came to mind.

"You'd do best to steer clear of her. Last I heard, her *vader* has been trying to get her married off."

Even hearing the word *marriage* made his stomach muscles tighten. A union such as that was now the furthest thing from his mind. It didn't matter what the young woman was like. Levi wasn't looking for a courtship anymore. The pain that his ex-fiancée, Anne Yoder, had put him through was still fresh in his mind and in his heart. Levi didn't think he would ever be able to bear the pain of a broken heart again.

He and Anne had seemed like the perfect match. Both of their families had agreed the marriage would be a good thing. But then Anne had abruptly changed her mind, leaving him for an *Englisch* man. No amount of talking to her had changed her mind. He felt badly for her *mudder* and *vader*. It was hard enough having a relationship end, but then to have their *dochder* leave the community… Well, he imagined that must have crushed their hearts.

As for Levi, he'd come to Miller's Crossing to work and to heal. Absently, he rubbed his hand over his belly as his stomach rumbled. He hadn't eaten much in the way of a meal since he'd left Fort Ann in the predawn hours this morning.

"You must be hungry after your day of travel. My wife, Rachel, is a *gut* cook. She'll have a hearty meal ready for us."

Levi had never met Rachel, although Jacob had talked about her at length the last time they'd been together.

Bright streaks of lightning slashed through the dark sky.

"Come, let's get to the house," Jacob shouted over the thunder.

Levi grabbed his travel bag from the back

of the wagon, and the two men dodged mud puddles as they ran to the safety of Jacob's house. Once on the porch, they shook the rain from their hats.

Jacob and Rachel's home looked good and sturdy. Built on a slight knoll overlooking the shed company, the house had dark wooden slat siding, and a grapevine wreath hung from the front door. Through the side windows, Levi could see soft light coming from the lamps hanging on the wall near the doors.

Jacob held the door open for him, and Levi stepped over the threshold into a great room that served as the kitchen, dining and living room. Off to one side was a large stove where a young woman wearing a white apron over a blue dress stood putting the finishing touches on their meal.

Jacob followed him into the house, saying, "Rachel, Levi is here."

Jacob's wife turned from the stove. Her smile was warm and kind. "*Willkomm* to our home. You made it to the house just in time. I fear this storm isn't going to let up any-time soon. You must be tired. After dinner, Jacob can show you to your room. We've a small bedroom you can use for as long as you need it."

"Levi, this is my wife, Rachel."

"*Sehr gut* to meet you." Levi nodded to her. "I've heard so much about you."

"Pleased to meet you, too. All of Jacob's family is *willkomm* in our home. Nodding her head in the direction of the table, she said, "Come, come, dinner is ready."

Rachel carried the steaming pot of stew to the table, then they took their seats.

Levi dug into the meal as Rachel and Jacob caught up on their day. It was obvious the couple loved one another. It occurred to him then that he might never get to experience this in his own life. He chided himself that this wasn't the time to worry about his future. He should concentrate on getting through the present. The exhaustion of the long day of travel had caught up with him, jumbling his thoughts.

Stifling a yawn, he thanked his hosts. "Rachel, *danke* for this meal. Jacob, if you don't mind, could you direct me to my room?"

"Ja. Ja," Jacob said, jumping up from his seat. "Right this way."

Levi picked up his travel bag from where he'd left it by the door and followed his friend down a long hallway toward the back of the house.

"Here is the room. I hope you find the bed to your liking."

"I'm sure I will." Levi was so tired he would be comfortable sleeping on a straw mat.

After Jacob left, Levi settled onto the single bed. He bent one arm under his head and lay there, listening to the storm. The thunder rumbled all around the house, sometimes so loud the windows rattled. He blinked into the darkness, holding his breath as he waited for the next strike of lightning. One hit close to the house, the flash illuminating the bedroom.

The storm rumbled away over the countryside. Then, just as it seemed that the storm had lost its fuel, it gathered energy once more and circled back around again. He hoped and prayed that the village wouldn't rise in the morning to find too much damage. After lying awake for a bit longer, he finally drifted off to sleep.

The sound of a voice calling his name jolted him awake, and thinking he was home, Levi shot out of the bed. By the time his feet hit the floor, he remembered where he was. The voice was not his *vader*'s but Jacob's.

Quickly, Levi got dressed and ran down the hall.

"Levi, come! We must hurry!"

Chapter Three

He met Jacob in the kitchen.

"I was out in the shop, and my workers came in and told me about storm damage throughout the area. We are going to head over to the schoolhouse. There's been a lot of damage there."

"Oh my! Sadie will be beside herself if something has happened to the school," Rachel said as she came up behind them.

Levi wondered what Sadie had to do with the schoolhouse. But there wasn't time to ask questions as they hurried outside into the early-morning light and hitched up one of Jacob's wagons, then joined the line of others on the main road heading toward Miller's Crossing.

Looking out from the wagon, Levi could

see where the storm had cut a path. Trees were felled in single rows along one of the hedgerows, and sirens were going off. They had to pull off onto the shoulder of the road to wait as an ambulance and fire truck sped past.

"I fear there's been a lot of damage, Levi."

"Me, too." He hung on tight as Jacob took the next corner at a good clip. "You were lucky your property was spared," Levi said.

"The storm circled around my house. I'm praying most of my neighbors have escaped any serious damage." Jacob pulled in the reins, slowing the horse's pace, and said, "The schoolhouse is up ahead."

Levi sat up taller, trying to catch a glimpse over the three wagons that had stopped on the side of the road just ahead of them. He let out a low whistle at the sight of what, by his best estimate, had to be a one-hundred-year-old oak tree split right down the middle. Half of it lay on the lawn in front of the long white schoolhouse. The other half was twisted in large sections. Large limbs had landed on an outbuilding and on top of the roof on a section of the one-story schoolhouse.

Hopping down, Jacob attached the reins

to a hitching post on the side of the graveled driveway. Levi followed him.

"Come on. Let's go see what we can do to help." Jacob led them over to the downed tree where a group of men had gathered. A few of them moved to the side to allow Jacob and Levi room to step in.

"I think we should break into groups," a tall man was saying. "One can start cutting the tree off the roof of the school and the others can see if the shed can be salvaged."

Out of the corner of his eye, Levi saw movement toward the back of the school building. Quietly he left the group to go investigate. There was no telling how safe the structures were under the weight of the trees, and he would hate to see someone get hurt. Pushing aside branches and stepping over twigs, he picked his way through the debris, coming to a stop around the backside of the schoolhouse.

He saw a flash of black. Was that a prayer *kapp*? A young woman raised her head, and there was no mistaking who she was.

Sadie Fischer.

Placing his hands on his hips, Levi looked at her. There were branches and twigs stuck all around her. He wondered how she even got in the spot to begin with. Even though she had tiny brown twigs sticking out from her hair, she looked a darn sight better than she had when he'd first met her yesterday. She lifted her head to look up at him, one hand holding a branch, the other shielding her face from the morning sun.

She narrowed her eyes. "Levi Byler, is that you?"

"Ja."

She frowned. "I don't need your rescuing today. As you can see, there's plenty of help to be had."

"I know that." Folding his arms, he widened his stance, trying to decide if he should help her out from the tangle of branches or go find someone else to help her.

She gave him a cross look, sucking in her lower lip as she wiggled around trying to find a way out of the brush pile.

"Ugh!"

"Geb acht!" Levi yelled.

Letting out a sigh, he dropped his arms and stepped toward her. If she wasn't careful, she would fall and get hurt. Levi was a stranger in these parts and there was no way he'd be accused of letting this woman get injured his first full day in town.

"Let me take hold of that branch and then you can slide out."

To his surprise, she did as told, letting the branch slip from her grasp into his hands. Once he felt certain it wouldn't spring back and hit her in the face, he let go and then reached for her. Of course, she pushed his hand away, stepping out of the branches on her own.

"Danke," she offered, brushing some leaves from her apron and pulling the twigs from her hair. "I can't believe the damage the storm brought. I came here with my *vader* to check on the building, and we were shocked to see all the trees that are down. And our *Englisch* neighbors had a tree come down on their car. I think they've lost power, too."

"It was a big storm."

"Some are saying it might have been a tornado. I'm not sure. What do you think?"

He shrugged, once again amazed at how quickly she could talk. "I think it's too soon to tell. Straight-line winds for sure." He tipped his head, looking her over. It was dangerous being out and about in the middle of broken tree limbs. "What are you doing back here by yourself?"

"I came to check on the flowers." Her

mouth dipping downward, she shuffled her feet along a brown patch of grass. "I think they are a total loss."

"Why would you be worrying about the flowers at a time like this?" He was more concerned about the building coming down around her.

"The *kinder* and I planted them at the end of the school year. The flowers were a special project." In the next breath, she asked, "Are you here to help out with the cleanup?"

"I came over with Jacob. Some of his workers were talking about this damage."

"Probably Abram Schmidt. I have two of his *kinder* in my class."

Levi tried to put this all together. Obviously, she cared about the school a great deal, otherwise she wouldn't be here worrying about the plants. Was she some sort of assistant? "You help out here at the school?"

Sadie pulled back her shoulders. "I do more than that, Mr. Byler. I'm the teacher here."

Levi's jaw dropped. He gave his head a shake in disbelief. But she had no reason to tell him otherwise. He frowned, trying to imagine her in a classroom as anything other than a student.

"You seem surprised."

Remembering his own teacher, who had been much older than Sadie and a lot more stern-looking, he offered, "Well, you just don't seem the type."

He didn't think it possible that she could narrow her eyes any more, but she managed. In a firm voice, she asked, "There's a type?"

Seeing he'd upset her, Levi held up his hands, gave her what he thought was a friendly grin and said, "You know what I mean."

Putting her hands on her hips, she glared up at him, her blue eyes filled with indignation.

"I don't know what you mean," she snapped.

Sadie had better things to do than stand here talking to this man. Why did he have to be the one to find her out here? She hadn't been all that stuck. Not like yesterday, anyway.

"Levi! There you are. We were wondering where you'd gotten off to," Jacob said as he came around the back of the building. And then he noticed Sadie. "Sadie! What are you doing back here?"

"Checking on the flower garden."

He wagged a finger at her. "You shouldn't be worrying over that."

She knew that, not when the school was in such a state. But her first thought had been for the children and how they'd worked so hard on this project. They'd been looking forward to seeing the fruits of their labor. If the garden could be saved, then they would have some hope.

Jacob said to Levi, "We were just dividing up the workload for the cleanup."

Sadie looked at Jacob, was thankful he'd saved her from any further chatting with Levi. To think he'd been surprised that she could be the schoolteacher. Sadie was well aware that pride goeth before the fall, but she was a *gut* teacher. She took her time smoothing down the folds of her dress, waiting for her temper to settle. It wouldn't do a bit of good to show her annoyance. Today was a day when everyone needed to work together, even if part of that everyone included Levi Byler.

She focused on Jacob. "*Gut.* The sooner we get this cleaned up, the sooner I can get on with preparing for the upcoming school year. We've only a few weeks until the first day," she reminded him.

"*Ja*, I know." Patting Levi on the back,

Jacob added, "Come on around to the front. We need to get you your assignment."

Sadie stayed a few steps behind as the three of them walked around to where Abram Schmidt was speaking.

"We're going to have the older boys remove the brush and smaller tree branches, while the men can cut the tree up into manageable lengths. The good news is the cleanup here will give us enough wood for next year's winter heating. The Lord does provide. And this will surely help with our next school budget.

"I think it best if we break up into three groups. One will work on getting the shed area cleared, one will work on the front and the other will see about damage to the school building," Abram went on.

Sadie looked around the lawn and noticed a few more buggies had pulled up in front. Some were loaded with saws and young men who'd come to help. Others carried women with baskets of food and thermoses. Confident the cleanup would be handled in a timely manner and knowing she wouldn't be needed there, Sadie headed off to join the women.

Rachel ran toward her. "Sadie!"

Sadie gave her a wave. "Rachel. *Gute mariye.*"

"*Ach*, I'm not sure how *gut* the morning is, what with all the damage in our community." Rachel wrinkled her nose.

"It is a *gute mariye* because no one was injured," Sadie reminded her.

Rachel gave her a thoughtful smile. "This is true. What do you think the damage is to the school?"

"I can't say for certain. I was out in the back hoping the flowers the *kinder* and I planted in the spring had survived. But I'm afraid all I saw were broken stems, and some of the plants were smushed underneath the tree limb that fell across the back."

"Those can be replanted," Rachel assured her.

"They can." Still, Sadie knew the *kinder* would be disappointed.

She linked her arm through Rachel's as they walked over to their friends. She said hello to a few of her students' *mamms* and was happy to see Lizzie Burkholder in the circle. Sadie broke away from Rachel to give Lizzie a hug.

"*Es dutt mir leed* my pot holders never made it to the store. I got myself into a bit of a mess while walking over."

Lizzie laughed. "You will have to tell me all about it."

"Well, let's just say it wasn't my finest moment."

Rachel came up to them. "Let's talk while we set up the food table. I see there are a few picnic tables we can use. You know how our men are. They will be hungry before you know it."

Sadie and Lizzie walked to where the tables had been set up in the side yard. They put out red-and-white-checked tablecloths as Sadie filled her friend in on yesterday's mess. Telling her how she'd taken the path behind the church and ended up stuck in the mud. By the time she'd finished recounting her day and how she'd been rescued by a stranger, the table was laden with sandwiches, salads and a big basket of apples.

Sadie kept her hands busy, but her mind was elsewhere. She was anxious to hear what the damage to the school might be and prayed they'd be able to open it in time for the new school year.

"Who is that man standing by Jacob?" Lizzie asked. "He keeps looking over this way."

Sadie glanced over her shoulder. Pulling

her mouth into a thin line, she answered, "That is Levi Byler."

"Your rescuer," Lizzie said, her eyes widening in curiosity. Nudging Sadie in the side with her elbow, she added, "He's headed this way."

Turning around to face him, Sadie figured he was coming for some food. She guessed he might not have had time for breakfast. His strides were long and purposeful as he crossed the lawn.

Levi stopped in front of her, and the gaggle of women behind her grew quiet. Sadie knew they were going to listen in. She had no desire to be fodder for their gossip. Squaring her shoulders, she tipped her head back to look up at him. He did not look happy at all. Of course, there was a lot of work to be done, and perhaps he was still tired from his long day yesterday. Either way, Sadie was beginning to think one of Rachel's egg salad sandwiches was not going to help his mood.

Sadie pasted her best smile on her face, the same one she used when a student became unruly. Folding her hands in front of her apron, she asked in a cheery voice, "Is there something I can help you with?"

Levi wasted no time with his answer. "It

appears that the work assignments have been given out."

A bad feeling wiggled along Sadie's spine. "I'm afraid I don't understand what that has to do with me."

"I am to work with the schoolteacher to get the schoolhouse ready for the new semester. And once that's done, I'll be overseeing the shed repair. Since you are the teacher, I guess this means you and I will be working together."

Sadie's jaw went slack.

Chapter Four

Behind her she heard an "oh" escape Rachel's mouth. Sadie didn't dare turn around. She knew Rachel and a few of the others must be grinning in delight over this turn of events. Her friends knew she was independent and enjoyed being in charge of her classroom. While she did have older students who helped with the lessons of the younger *kinder*, the setting up and running of the schoolroom fell to her.

Having to work side by side with this stranger would be a challenge for sure, even if he was a relative of Jacob's. She decided it was best to remain professional. After all, she was the teacher and she wanted the best for her students. Her discomfort over the matter shouldn't be of any concern.

Except that feeling didn't seem like it would be going away anytime soon.

Sadie blew out a breath, then said, "Well, why don't you grab something to eat, and after that, we'll take a look at the damage and make a list of what needs to be done in order to get the school fixed."

She followed him to the food table and did the neighborly thing by introducing him to the women who'd cooked the food. They piled his plate high with an egg salad sandwich and spoonfuls of two kinds of potato salad, along with a generous helping of her own *mamm*'s locally famous macaroni salad. A smile tugged at her mouth when she saw Rachel add a large chocolate chip cookie. She wasn't sure Levi would be able to eat everything.

But he managed. After he finished, he tossed his empty paper plate and utensils in a nearby trash can and gave her a half smile. "Shall we go take stock of what needs to be fixed?"

Nodding, Sadie couldn't help thinking again that Levi Byler needed to smile more. Smiles had a way of warming one's soul. From his stiff demeanor, she had a feeling Levi's soul was in need of some warmth. She walked ahead of him, leading the way to the front door of the schoolhouse, which was ajar.

As she stepped over the threshold, her breath caught in her throat, and her hand covered her heart. "Oh my," she breathed at the sight before them.

Shards of glass littered the floor where a window on the left side had been broken by a tree limb. The wood floor had puddles of water clear to the center of the room. Some of the educational posters on the wall had blown off and were lying in the water. One of the green blackout shades flapped in the breeze against the broken window.

Sadie paused to send up a fervent prayer of thanks that all her students had been safe in their homes when the disaster hit. This damage could be fixed.

Still, a sadness filled her. It was difficult to see the classroom that she'd grown to love and take comfort in looking such a mess. The storm had been ferocious. Sadie knew in her heart this all could have been so much more devastating.

Bending down, she picked up a paperback book that had fallen off a shelf. Setting the soggy mess on a desk she was standing next to, she turned to look at Levi. He, too, stood taking in the storm damage. Her gaze followed his up to a basketball-size hole in the roof. She could see clear out to the sky, now blue. They'd need to get a tarp on that right away.

Looking down at her, he said, "It could have been worse."

"Ja," she agreed, as he gave voice to her thoughts. "At least it's not a total loss like the shed appears to be."

When she'd gone out earlier to check on the garden, she'd carefully avoided what was left of the shed. They'd kept the garden supplies and some of the playground equipment out there, but all of that could be replaced.

She picked her way through the debris. Walking over to her desk, she found a notebook and a pen. Picking them up, she started making a list of what needed to be done. First off, *clean up.* Then *fix the window.* She was about to add *replace torn posters and damaged books* when Levi approached her.

"I'm going to see if anyone has a tarp stored in their wagon. At least we can get that hole covered up until we get the supplies needed to fix it."

"That sounds like a *gut* idea," Sadie replied. "Then we can work on the rest of the list."

He raised an eyebrow.

"Is there something the matter?"

He shook his head.

Twirling the pen between her fingers, she kept her tone even as she said, "Please don't tell me you have a problem with making lists."

Sadie, for one, liked lists. They kept her on track. Maybe Levi was the type of person who kept everything in his head.

"I don't. You give me what you come up with and I'll see that whatever is on there gets taken care of."

"Mr. Byler, I'm perfectly capable of helping out here. I know the students and what needs to be in place before they return in a few weeks for the start of the fall semester. It makes sense that I handle getting the ruined classroom supplies replaced. Besides, you're going to be very busy working on the building." Softening her tone, she added, "Unless you think you'll have time to go to the King's Office Supply and Bookstore to pick up what I'll need."

While she waited for his reply, Sadie looked beyond him, once again surveying the mess caused by the storm, only now seeing the torn strip of paper hanging from the wall. One of her most loved quotes:

> Be Kind, Be Thoughtful, Be Genuine,
> But Most Of All, Be Thankful

Reading that reminded her she should be thankful for all of the help here today, including Levi Byler's.

It also reminded her that she loved this building and what it represented. Here was where the *kinder* came to learn not only their numbers and letters but how to be kind. She taught them about their faith, forgiveness and how to work together. They also practiced the Golden Rule, to treat others as you would want to be treated.

It pained her to see even one thing out of place. The *kinder* she taught were part of her community. Many were a part of her family. They deserved to come back to a building that had been repaired to its fullest potential. She owed it to them to see that that happened.

Besides, she didn't want to disappoint the school board either. It had been hard enough convincing them she was the right person for the job. It wouldn't do to have some storm come through and prove otherwise.

She knew full well the men of this community were strong, but the women could be counted on, too. Sadie could find a way for her and Levi to work together.

Levi watched various emotions play out on Sadie's face. Her expression had gone from determination to sadness and finally to acceptance. He didn't want to waste time arguing with her, but this project was the first one for him as Jacob's helper and he wanted it to go well. He had to make this work. It shouldn't be too bad. Obviously, this teacher wanted what was best for her students, as did he.

Of course, his way of tackling a project wasn't necessarily making lists. He liked to get a feel for a job before stepping into it. He got the idea that Sadie wanted to get her lists made and then dole out the tasks.

Being a stranger to this community didn't make his job any easier. He didn't mind helping where help was needed, even if repairing the school hadn't been the reason he'd come to Miller's Crossing. But you never knew what life was going to hand you.

Levi came close to letting out a snort at that last thought. Life certainly hadn't gone the way he'd planned. He should have been married by now, setting up a home with the woman he loved. But the Lord had other plans. Levi knew better than to try to interpret what those might be. He had to trust in the Lord.

Letting those thoughts tumble from his mind, he looked at Sadie.

She had gone back to writing on her notepad. From the way her hand had moved three quarters of the way down the page, he surmised the list had grown a bit longer.

He realized that she would know better than he what needed to be replaced. Looking around, he took in the larger damage. The broken window, the hole in the roof. That roof damage in and of itself could lead to more work. He wouldn't know until he got up there how many shingles were damaged. And he had no idea about the books and other things that needed to be replaced.

Putting his hands on his hips, he said, "I think you are right. It would be best if you took care of going to the office supply and bookstore."

"Danke."

He noticed a wisp of her blond hair had fallen from underneath her prayer *kapp*. She caught his gaze on her. Lifting her hand, she tucked the strand back in place. A light blush rose high on her cheekbones.

Levi looked down at the desktop. "Tell me what else you have on your list."

"Cleaning up the storm debris will be first because we won't know the full extent of the damage until we can see underneath everything. Then we'll need to clear out this room so we can scrub and paint." Letting out an exasperated sigh, she added, "There's so much to see to. I'm not sure this can all be done in a few weeks."

"There is a lot of help waiting right outside those doors," he said, pointing over his shoulder at the group of men, both old and young, who had come out to assist.

"Yes. You are right. I'm overreacting."

He shook his head. "*Nee*. This mess is hard to look at. But we'll all work to get everything fixed, and it will be better than before."

The schoolteacher gave him a smile.

Levi simply nodded in return. "All right then. It seems like we're making headway."

"We are. Do you think you could call

some of those helpers inside to start moving things?"

Levi left her at her desk and walked outside to find Jacob. On his way over to the men, he noticed that more tables had been added to the area where he'd eaten earlier, forming a long row of communal seating. Someone had erected a blue pop-up canopy to cover the food, and it ruffled in the warm breeze.

He met Jacob in the front yard. "Sadie and I have come up with a plan for the schoolhouse."

"I'm glad to hear that," Jacob replied. "We've given our groups their tasks. We're lucky enough that some of the older students have come by to assist. I think they should work with you and Sadie."

Levi nodded. It would be *gut* for the boys to help rebuild their own school. "I think the first order of business is to get a tarp up on the roof," Levi advised.

"*Ja.* I looked in the wagons that are here and didn't find any. You should go into the village and pick one up at the hardware store. I've an account there for my business. You can tell him you're my cousin and you have my permission to add the purchases to my account. And let Herb, the owner, know that I'll be in at the end of the week to settle as usual."

"I can do that. Is the tarp all we'll be needing?"

"Why don't you pick up extra tarps? We can use them to cover up the school desks and other items that Sadie wants protected. I have some boxes over at my shop that we can put the books and supplies in. And I think among the men who came today, we have enough supplies to begin the cleanup."

Jacob and Levi agreed to have the crews start removing the tree limbs from around the school first, and then they would take the portion of the trunk off the roof. Jacob took his tools out of his wagon and then told Levi to use that to go into town.

"If you think of anything else we might need, don't hesitate to buy it," Jacob told him as Levi climbed up onto the seat.

"Would you mind telling me the best way to get to the village?"

"Sure! Turn left at the first intersection and then go two more intersections. You'll see the sign pointing the way to Clymer. Go through the stoplight and you'll find the hardware store in the next block."

"Danke."

Levi set off the way Jacob instructed. Here and there along the way were signs of storm damage. A tree had fallen into a portion of the road, causing him to maneuver the horse onto the opposite side. When he came to the first intersection, he waited for a pickup truck and two cars to go through before proceeding.

Eventually he made it into the village and parked the wagon next to a small hitching post. Hopping down from his seat, he took a look around. Clymer was a quaint village. He noticed the hardware store and bank, and down the road he spotted a three-story, redbrick schoolhouse. This one was for the *Englisch kinder.* At the main intersection, he noticed the grocery store. Good to remember in case he needed any sundry items. He also saw the storefront for Burkholder's Amish Furniture and Art store. A really nice dining table and bench set were displayed in the window.

The door opened and a couple came out. The man was tall and carried some sort of canvas. At first Levi wasn't sure why the couple held his attention, and then it dawned on him that the woman looked very familiar. Her dark hair and her height, the angle of her jaw. She looked just like his former fiancée.

Levi didn't think it could be possible for her to be so close to Miller's Crossing. This woman wasn't wearing dark skirts and a prayer *kapp.* She was dressed in blue jeans with a sleeveless white top tucked into the waistband.

Shock rolled through him as he stared at the woman he'd once thought he loved. *What is she doing here?*

Chapter Five

"Anne?" he whispered.

The woman looked across the street, their gazes colliding, and he realized it wasn't her. Upon seeing him, an Amish man, the woman quickly reached into her pocketbook. She pulled out her cell phone and held it at arm's length, pointing it at him, and quickly tapped her finger on the screen. He ducked his head, hoping to avoid having his picture taken. Though he felt certain she'd managed to capture his image.

Levi's knees went weak with relief as he realized this woman was nothing more than just another *Englisch* tourist. Still, his breathing was quick and shallow. He kept his head bowed as he tried to absorb the pain that tore through his heart. He'd been trying for weeks to shut that part of his life off. And today, in this very minute, like the ripples of water lapping against a shoreline, the sadness washed over him. He kept his head downturned and swallowed against the tightness gripping his throat like a vise.

Taking in a breath, he waited for the tightness to ease. He exhaled, concentrating on the ache in his chest. Levi knew a few deep breaths wouldn't fix what ailed him. He wanted this feeling of hurt and betrayal to be gone. There was no place in his life or in his heart now for it, and yet for the moment the unbearable pain crippled him.

He stood on the side of the road with life's noises in the background. Car horns and kids playing in their backyards filtered through the fogginess of his brain. He knew deep in his soul that Anne had made her choice. He'd accepted that. She had moved on and he'd chosen to come to Miller's Crossing to help his cousin, with the possibility of maybe starting fresh.

He heard a car door close, then an engine start, and he lifted his head, looking up as the two tourists drove off. Squaring his shoulders, Levi pushed his pain back down and entered the hardware store.

Within seconds, an *Englisch* man came over to ask if he needed assistance. Levi asked for a tarp large enough to cover the hole in the roof at the Amish school in Miller's Crossing. The man, whose nametag read Herb, led him to the back of the store.

"Wow, this shelf is almost empty. I guess with the storm we've had a lot of people come in needing these," the man observed. Pulling a large blue tarp off the top shelf, he handed it to Levi.

Levi noticed right away that it was the last one. "I don't need to take this if there's a chance someone else might come in with a hole in the roof of their home."

"Thanks for the offer, but we have an order coming in tomorrow morning. The storm damage in some sections of Clymer is pretty intense," Herb said. "Can I get you anything else?"

"*Ja*, I'll add a couple cases of roofing shingles and nails." It wouldn't hurt to have them in case they were able to get started on the repair today.

He followed the man down another aisle, where they picked up the supplies. Back at the checkout counter, Levi told Herb this would go on his cousin Jacob's account. Herb seemed fine with that, looked up the information and then rang up the items. He printed out two receipts, handed one to Levi and put the other inside a ledger.

"If you need us to deliver any more supplies, just let me know."

"*Danke.* I'll tell Jacob."

"Do you have a wagon outside?"

"I do."

"Well, let me help you get this stuff loaded up."

Hefting one of the boxes of shingles onto his shoulder, Herb followed Levi outside and set it in the back of the wagon. Once everything was loaded, Levi headed back to the schoolyard. He imagined the crew would be about ready to get the tarp in place.

He was amazed at the amount of work that had been done in the two hours he'd been gone. The tree had been removed from the schoolhouse, and the older students had already started cutting the wood into smaller sections. Even from the driveway he could see a decent-size hole in the midsection of the roof. The tarp would cover that nicely until they could get back up there tomorrow. He parked the wagon with the others.

Jacob saw him drive in and came over to help unload.

"Looks like you've been busy," Levi commented.

"It's nice the older schoolboys are helping out. I think being a part of working on something that's for the good of the community keeps them grounded."

Levi agreed. When he was a young lad, he'd enjoyed working on community projects. It made him feel like he belonged to a larger family.

Hefting the heavy shingles onto one shoulder, he headed off toward the front of the schoolhouse, where he dropped the heavy shingles to the ground. Looking up, he noticed Sadie standing in the doorway speaking to a man he hadn't met. He appeared to be much older than her. With a gray beard and gray hair, the man stood with a slight hunch in his shoulders.

Sadie had her arms folded in front of her, and she wasn't smiling. As a matter of fact, he thought there might even be a scowl on her face. He wondered if the man was someone she didn't like.

Taking a handkerchief out of his pants pocket, Levi brushed the brim of his straw hat back and wiped the sweat from his forehead. The storm that had plowed through last night had left behind air thick with heat and humidity. The sweat seeped through his work shirt. Tucking the cloth back into his pocket, he walked over to the entrance. He was anxious to see what the interior looked like now that some of the debris had been cleared.

Sadie stood on the top step watching Levi's approach over the top of the man's head. Levi couldn't decide if the man was a relative or a neighbor. He overheard a portion of what the man was saying.

"I'm sorry I didn't come last night. The storm came in so fast."

"*Ja*. That it did."

Levi thought Sadie sounded agitated. He wondered why.

"Your *daed* was kind enough to invite me back to dinner on another night," the man spoke softly, shifting his weight from one foot to the other.

"Then I'll see you on that night," Sadie replied in a dismissive tone.

Levi took that moment to step up to them. "Hello," he said to the man.

With a half smile, the man met Levi's gaze

and stuck his hand out to shake. "I'm Isaiah Troyer."

"Levi Byler."

"New to the area?"

"I'm here to help my cousin Jacob Hershberger with his shed company." Looking around, Levi added, "And to help with these repairs."

"I imagine the storm caught you a bit off guard."

"It was a rough night."

"And now you are helping out here. *Gut* sturdy men can be hard to find. The community is fortunate you came to visit when you did," Isaiah said with a tip of his hat. "There seems to be enough help here and I've got work to do at home." Turning his attention back to Sadie, he said, "I hope to see you again soon."

Sadie nodded, spun on her heel and went inside. Again, Levi couldn't be certain, but it seemed that she really didn't like that man. Following her inside, he paused and looked around in surprise. The desks had all been moved to one side of the room and the bookcases were nearly emptied out, with the books stacked in cardboard boxes. The exposed hole in the roof brought in a lot of sunlight. That would be covered shortly.

The green blackout shades had been removed from all but one window in the back of the classroom. Sadie was working at getting the rest of the posters down and rolled up to be stored away. The side walls were bare, and there were still three left behind her desk on either side of the chalkboard.

He let out a short whistle. "You've been busy!"

Sadie shook her head. "I didn't do this alone. I had plenty of help."

"This is a *gut* start."

"It is. I'm thankful for all the students who've come by. And the *mudders* have restocked the food table twice now," Sadie said with a laugh. "If you're hungry, you can go out and grab something."

"I'm *gut*," Levi told her.

She noticed the sweat on his brow and seeping through his shirt. Even she was feeling the heaviness of the humidity and had gone out a few minutes ago to get herself something cold to drink.

"How about a lemonade?" she asked.

"I can get one if I'm thirsty."

"Okay," she said. *Suit yourself.* She turned around to look at what was left of the posters on the wall. She reached up to take the one with the alphabet down from behind her desk. Except the tack on the top right side held firm. Her first instinct was to give it a tug, but she didn't want to tear it. Instead she grabbed for the back of her desk chair, planning to stand on it, but jumped when she felt a warm hand on hers.

She hadn't heard Levi come over. She spun around and looked up, ready to offer him a thankful smile. Except he stood scowling down at her. She bit her lower lip and wondered why he acted as though he didn't like her. Maybe she was being too judgmental. She did her best to be kind to everyone, including Isaiah Troyer. Of course, if she were honest, she did not want to do anything to make that man think there would be a union between the two of them.

His arrival here today indicated that he genuinely wanted to help out. This school was a part of his community. But the last thing she needed right now was a distraction. She wanted to concentrate on restoring her school.

"I can get this down," Levi said. "No need for you to climb up on the chair."

Stepping aside, she let Levi remove the last three posters. After rolling and wrapping a rubber band around each one, she gathered them up and placed them in the last open box. With that done, she only had to get the desks moved to the basement and the last green shade down. Then she could think about cleaning the room so they could repair, repaint and reopen in time for her to teach the three R's. Sadie let out a laugh.

Levi looked at her. "What's so funny?"

"Nothing. A silly thought I had, that's all. *Danke* for helping me get those posters down. Now I can move the desks downstairs, and we can begin the hard work."

"You know the menfolk can handle this."

"I do, but it's still my classroom. I'm able to use a paint roller and wipe a window clean."

"I'm sure you are. But you can't do any of those things until we have the repairs finished. By my best estimation, that will be sometime next week."

Sadie did her own calculation, determining they had exactly three weeks to get everything done. Two weeks to do the repairs would leave her with a week to get the classroom set up and ready for the new school semester. "That should work."

"Keep in mind, Sadie, that we still don't know the extent of the roof damage."

"Speaking of the roof," Jacob said as he strode into the classroom, "we've got a ladder so we can get up there, take a closer look and get the tarp on before nightfall."

Coming around from behind the desk, Levi joined Jacob, saying, "All right then, let's go."

The three of them went outside. Sadie stood off to one side. Raising her hand to shield her eyes from the brightness of the sun, she watched while the men took turns climbing up the ladder. Jacob yelled down for someone to bring up the tarp. Once that was done, they covered the hole. She ran her hand along her forehead to wipe the beads of perspiration away.

Someone bumped into her elbow, and Sadie smiled when she turned and saw Lizzie.

"Lizzie!" Sadie gave her friend a big hug.

"This heat is getting to me. Why don't you come over to the tent and have something cold to drink? I made my pink lemonade."

Sadie loved seeing her dear friend so happy. Lizzie's transformation had been nothing short of a miracle. Ever since marrying Paul Burkholder, she'd been beaming. Right now, she was smiling from ear to ear. Even the scar that had marred her dear friend's face since the childhood accident that took her *bruder*'s life had faded into nothing more than a barely noticeable thin line.

"Let's go get that drink," Sadie said, sliding her arm through Lizzie's. She wouldn't tell her that she'd just had one. On a day like this, a person couldn't get enough to drink.

"This storm left behind a lot of humidity."

"That it did. Maybe tomorrow will be better for working outside."

"I know we shouldn't be complaining." Lizzie laughed.

They walked across the schoolyard to the shady area where the tents and tables were set up. The women were busy doling out the last of the salads and sandwiches from the coolers. Sadie knew they'd be refilled and brought back tomorrow. She let Lizzie lead her to the drink table, where Lizzie handed her a glass of the cold lemonade. Bringing the paper cup to her lips, she drank in the mixture of tart sweetness. Always a perfect fix to the heat.

Sadie turned and looked out over the yard. She could see the area where the *kinder* played kickball. Beyond that were the swing set and slide. Branches and twigs littered the area. But that would all be gone in a few days.

"Tell me how things are going." Lizzie picked up a drink and stood beside Sadie.

"We accomplished a lot today. And I feel that tomorrow, with the desks cleared and the books packed away, the men can get in and fix the window. There are a few spots in the one wall that need to be patched."

"I saw Isaiah Troyer earlier."

Sadie swallowed a mouthful of lemonade. She concentrated on watching the men put away their tools for the day. She wasn't sure how much Lizzie knew about the situation. But she had to talk to someone about her feelings.

"*Ja.* He came by to check on me."

"That was nice of him, don't you think?" Lizzie asked, keeping her voice low so the other women couldn't hear them.

"What I think is that he is too old for me."

"He's the man your *vader* has chosen."

"He is, but my *vader* understands my feelings on this matter."

Lizzie looked at her sympathetically. "He can understand, but do you think it will make any difference?"

Sadie shrugged. "You know how I feel about finding the right man."

Lizzie's face softened with laughter. Her

eyes lit up as she chuckled, recited Sadie's very thoughts on the matter. "He can't be too old or too young. He has to be your perfect Amish man."

They burst out laughing. Someone cleared their throat. Sadie swung her head around and came face-to-face with Levi Byler.

Chapter Six

She heard Lizzie's surprised intake of breath. Her own seemed caught in her throat.

Oh my goodness!

Sadie could only imagine what Levi must be thinking of her now. Although if the deep frown he wore was any indication, she might think he didn't approve of her requirements for a husband.

At that moment, Sadie couldn't help wondering if perhaps she was turning into one of those women who simply couldn't make up their minds about things like this. *Nee.* She knew what she wanted. Lizzie's words were Sadie's truth.

She coughed, then asked, "Are the men done for the day?"

"They are. Everyone is packing up and

heading home. Most of them have evening chores that need tending to," he answered, avoiding making eye contact with her.

Sadie felt bad that he'd overheard a conversation between two lifelong friends. Friends who very rarely kept things from one another.

"Well, Lizzie and I are going to help pack up here and then we'll be heading to our homes, too."

"Okay. Will you need a ride?"

She shook her head. "My *vader* is right over there." She pointed behind Levi to the place in the yard where her *vader* had pulled the family wagon in line with the others a few minutes ago.

"I'll see you tomorrow."

"I'll be here bright and early," Sadie quipped, giving Levi her best smile.

She watched him walk off, then turned to help with the last of the packing up. Lizzie was bent over a large red cooler, putting away empty plastic containers. Sadie joined her, handing her the last three left on the picnic table.

"I take it he heard what I said?" Lizzie wanted to know.

"I'm afraid so."

"You don't seem too upset by that."

"I'm not. He didn't mention our conversation, but I could tell by the look on his face that he'd heard us. I don't know Levi all that well. But from what I've seen so far, he tries to keep to himself."

Lizzie shrugged. "Maybe that will change as he gets to know us all better. He is Jacob's cousin, so he does have some family here. I'm sure once he settles in, he'll get more comfortable."

"Maybe." But even as she agreed, Sadie had a feeling Levi just might not be the outgoing type.

After saying her goodbyes to Lizzie and the other women who'd been helping out under the food tent, Sadie went to meet her *vader*. He was waiting for her in the shade of a stand of maple trees. She waved at him. When he saw her coming toward him, he smiled at her.

"Good afternoon, *dochder*."

"Good afternoon, *vader*."

Nodding in the direction of their wagon, he walked with her over to where he'd parked it. "Did the day go well?"

"*Ja*. The men came out in full force. Tomorrow we can start repairing the inside of the schoolhouse."

Sadie caught him looking beyond her to

where Levi and Jacob were getting into Jacob's wagon. Both men looked flushed from the heat and tired.

Sadie rubbed a hand along her face, feeling the warmth of her skin beneath her fingertips. The humidity had spiked. She prayed there wouldn't be another storm tonight. Unfortunately, this was the time of the year for them. She'd long gotten over her childhood fear of late-night storms and the thunder and lightning that came with them. The crops needed the rain.

"This cousin of Jacob's, did he help out today?"

Sadie gave a start at his question. It was interesting that her *vader* wanted to know about Levi. *"Ja."* She thought it best to leave her answer at that.

Her *vader* wanted a union between her and Isaiah Troyer. Sadie knew that wasn't going to happen. She feared her *vader* might be upset if he knew she was working with Levi Byler. Being the schoolteacher, her life required a different set of proprieties. She had a reputation to keep. Even though they were working among a lot of other community members, her *vader* might frown upon their partnership.

However, the only thing that concerned her

was getting the school up and running in time for the new semester. She didn't care how that came about.

Settling herself onto the seat of the wagon, Sadie adjusted her blue skirt. The toll of putting in a long day's work was catching up with her. Her shoulders ached from moving the desks, and her feet felt as if they might explode out of her shoes. She couldn't wait to get her shoes and stockings off. She wiggled her toes in anticipation. As they rode past the white schoolhouse, she saw the blue tarp flattened against the roof covering the hole. She sent up a prayer of thanksgiving that today had gone well and that the Lord had sent an extra pair of hands in the form of Levi Byler.

"Did you happen to see Isaiah?" her *vader* asked.

"He came by to check on me," Sadie admitted.

"Gut."

"Vader—" she started, wanting to tell him to stop wasting his time and effort on something that would not happen.

His stern voice interrupted her. "*Dochder*, you have no idea how I wish you would abide by my decision concerning you and Isaiah."

"I understand."

He slapped the leather reins against the backside of the large mare pulling the wagon. "I'm not sure you do."

"Can't you please give me a little more time?" Sadie asked softly.

A breeze blew in from the north, bringing with it a hint of coolness. Sadie lifted her face, letting the air wash over her. She waited for an answer from her *vader*, hoping he would continue to allow her lenience in this matter.

"I know you're going to be busy at the school, and that's where your attention should be. The community needs you there. But that doesn't mean I'll be forgetting about my wishes where your future is concerned."

Sadie looked over at her *vader*. His jaw was set in that stubborn way he had when he was mad.

She didn't want him to be angry with her over this. There was too much at stake. Her future, for one. And her heart. She couldn't waste either on a man she would never love. She knew there were plenty of marriages built on love. Jacob and Rachel, and Lizzie and Paul came to mind. They'd all overcome obstacles, but in the end, they'd found their true love. That was all she wanted.

Blowing out a breath, she wondered if that kind of love was even in the Lord's plans for her.

A week later Levi stood in the schoolyard, the early dawn light casting soft shadows from the trees onto the lawn. The air was still and quiet. He liked working in solitude, without distraction. On his way here, he'd seen deer drinking out of a stream and red-winged blackbirds perched on the fence that ran along Jacob's property. The early-morning hours were the perfect time to reflect and meditate on the good word.

Unfortunately, some of today's thoughts were filled with words he'd overheard Sadie and her friend saying last week.

He found it interesting that she was so set on knowing what she wanted for every part of her life. Like how she wanted the classroom to look when it was finished and what she wanted in a husband. Mind you, none of the latter was any of his business, but he'd heard her words and there was no forgetting them.

Levi wanted to tell her, based on his life experience thus far, that there was no such thing as a "perfect" person, be they Amish or otherwise. Every last one of them had been born with flaws. It didn't take much to remind him the reason he was here had nothing to do with finding a proper wife and everything to do with putting his hands to work. Busy hands kept one's mind from wandering back to the past.

Of course, he could have stayed in his community. If not for Jacob's offer of employment, he might have done just that. Levi was a strong person. But he hadn't expected the turn his life took a few months ago to leave him feeling so unsettled. His *mamm* had been the one to encourage him to make a change. She'd seen the pain Anne's betrayal had caused and had told Levi a new start could be what he needed. Coming here to Miller's Crossing had seemed like the right thing to do.

Bringing his mind back to the task at hand, he rubbed his hands together, feeling a blister on the inside of his right thumb. It was his own fault. The preceding days had been filled with many tasks, and he hadn't been wearing the work gloves Jacob had given him. He'd been hammering away on the shingles, replacing some of the wood siding and even helping chop a bit of wood.

Levi rolled the ache out of his shoulders,

aware of the heat. Not even nine o'clock and the August day was growing hot. He'd been in the schoolyard since sunup, hoping to get ahead of the workload. Swiping his sleeve across his brow, he walked around the back of the schoolhouse to take a look at where the shed once stood. He knew it would be at least two more days before he could get started out here, but he wanted to get an idea of the size of the original foundation.

He did a quick pace of the area. Walking heel-to-toe along the remaining slab, he estimated the structure had been sixteen by twelve feet. A decent size for storage.

Jacob had told him this morning that he didn't have a shed of this size in stock. They would have to build it from scratch. He also suggested that rather than constructing it at the shed company, they should work here, on-site. This would save them in shipping costs since Jacob contracted with a local transport company to deliver the sheds.

Levi wanted to get this project done. Then he could begin working with Jacob on his business. The shed company was doing really well, and he knew Jacob was anxious to expand. Levi wanted to support him.

Meanwhile, it was time to start repainting

the walls inside the school. He said hello to one of the women who still came by to help with the food tent, which had decreased in size as fewer workers were needed. But the food and drinks were still welcomed by the remaining crew.

He walked along the side of the school, noticing how the new clapboards blended in with the old. The windows were open, letting in the summer breeze, and he caught a glimpse of Sadie inside talking to some of her students. He recognized an older boy from earlier this week.

"Miss Sadie, my *vader* said I should work with you today," the tall, lanky boy was saying.

"Thank you so much, Jeremiah. It's very kind of him to allow you to be here. We're going to start painting!"

Levi heard the excitement in her voice. He walked through the tall blades of grass and made his way around to the front door. Entering the room, he noticed that Sadie was indeed ready for painting. She had on a light blue skirt and matching blouse covered by a canvas work apron. Her hair was neatly tucked up under her prayer *kapp*. Three five-gallon pails of flat-white paint sat near the door, along with four rolls of blue painter's tape, paint pans, rollers and paintbrushes.

Surveying the room, he thought it might take the three of them the better part of a day to get this job done. He was pleased when a few others in the community straggled in. That meant he would be freed up to begin work on the shed.

"Mica! Josh! *Danke* for coming today," Sadie greeted the newcomers. Then turning to Levi, she explained, "I asked Josh Troyer and his friend Mica King to help us out, too. I hope you don't mind."

Seeing her delight in getting extra help made him realize that Sadie could be extremely resourceful.

"More hands make less work for us," he commented.

"That's what I was thinking. We should start by taping off all of the windows. Then we can get the paint on the walls. Once that is done, I can have the men help bring the desks up from the basement. Then we can get everything back in place. The room is going to look the nicest it's ever been when we are finished. The students deserve a clean, safe place for their learning. Don't you agree, Levi?"

His head was spinning over all the words

she managed to get out in a few seconds. He started to answer her, but she began talking again.

"As soon as the paint dries, we can bring the posters back out and get them hung up and get the shades back up on the windows. And then I can start hauling in the boxes of books. I still have to get over to the stationery store to pick up the replacements for the books that were damaged. I'm so excited, Levi—it's looking like we'll be done on time."

"That it does. You're a good worker."

He didn't know why he said that. She was a *good worker.* That sounded so impersonal, like he was speaking to one of the men. But his compliment brought a light blush to her cheekbones, and Levi found himself wanting to smile.

"*Danke.* I just want everything to be perfect for the students."

"With your enthusiasm, I'm certain that it will be."

Mesmerized by the sparkle of hope reflected in her blue eyes, Levi found it hard to look away. But it appeared that she had her mind set on getting today's work started, and her attention quickly shifted from him to the young man standing next to her.

"The first thing we need to do is get the blue tape around the door and window frames," she said to Jeremiah. "Why don't you help me get that started?"

Eager to please, the young man's head bobbed up and down so hard, his hat nearly tumbled from his head. He managed to catch it in time as he followed his teacher over to the pile of supplies stacked near the door. Sadie pulled the protective plastic wrap off the rolls of tape and handed one to Jeremiah.

"Since you're one of the tallest, let's have you start with the entry door."

Jeremiah's reach went almost to the top of the doorframe.

Levi stopped him.

"Wait. Don't overreach or you'll end up hurting your back. Let me go find a ladder for you, Jeremiah."

Levi went outside and brought back in a five-step ladder. Setting it up, he said, "Watch your step, and don't go above the fourth rung."

Words from the instructor at the Ladders Last safety seminar he and Jacob had attended together in Saratoga last year came back to him. He never imagined he'd be using the lesson at a school. But, he supposed, *gut* advice could be put to use in just about any situation.

Confident that Jeremiah could handle the job, Levi grabbed a roll and began taping around the windows. Sadie worked along the floor and walls.

It took the better part of the morning to get all the tape up. Even though it was a pain to do, it would save them the time scraping the windowpanes and floorboards afterward.

Eventually, he heard a soft groan coming from the other side of the room and turned to see Sadie getting up from her hands and knees. Rushing over, he offered her his hand.

At first, he thought she was going to push him away, but then she took hold of his hand, saying, "*Danke.* I was down here far too long without a break."

He helped her into a standing position.

Sadie blew out a breath. "*Phew!* I'm glad that's done. Now we can get the canvas cloths on the floor and start this project."

Letting go of her hand, Levi followed her to the other side of the room. Together they unfurled the heavy canvas and laid the cloth out on the floor. Grabbing a steel tool that looked a lot like a can opener, he ran the tip of it around the rim of the first five-gallon bucket of paint. Setting the opener on the canvas, he carefully lifted the lid. The color was a simple off-white.

Peering over his shoulder, Sadie observed, "I really wanted a yellow for the new color. But they didn't have any and I didn't want to make the cost go higher by mixing a custom color."

Sitting back on his haunches, he looked up at her curiously. "Is yellow a favorite color of yours?"

She gave him a soft smile, nodding. "*Ja.* It reminds me of sunshine. But it's frivolous to have that here when most of the walls are covered with posters and bookshelves. Do you have a favorite color, Levi?"

Grabbing the handle of the paint bucket, he carefully tipped some into a heavy metal tray. He'd never really given color much thought. Most of his life had been surrounded by the simple colors of their clothing.

Concentrating on getting the paint into the tray and not onto the floor covering, he answered, "I suppose I favor blue."

"There are so many shades of blue."

He paused and said, "I like the color of the

sky." *And your eyes.* He thought Sadie's eyes were about the prettiest blue he'd ever seen.

"*Ja.* The sky is pretty most days. Unless it's storming. But even then, it can be beautiful." Sadie's voice took on a wistful tone.

"We'd best concentrate on our work."

He stood, picked up the package of rollers and pulled them out. Placing one on a handle, he showed the boys how to glide the paint roller along the bottom of the flat metal pan.

"You don't want to get too much or else you'll have drips running down the walls," he advised.

Sadie nodded, adding, "And if you don't get enough, then you'll have dry patches. We can't have that. Here, let me show you."

Reaching down, she took hold of one of the rollers and gently slid it into the pan. Once she had enough white paint, she moved the roller up and down on the wall.

"See how I'm making a W shape and how you're getting a lesson at the same time!" Sadie let out a laugh. "After you make that letter, you go back and fill in the space. Like this."

"This way you'll get a nice even coat," Levi finished, impressed with her painting skills.

"That's it exactly," Sadie agreed, smiling at him.

He felt the corners of his mouth turn upward and quickly busied himself with gathering a brush and container to pour some paint into. He didn't want to be drawn to Sadie, and yet he was finding it harder and harder to resist her charm. Turning away from everyone else, Levi began applying paint to the baseboard trim along the floor.

It wasn't long before he heard the light, sweet sound of someone humming. Sadie. Her voice sounded so lyrical. Levi listened to her hum one of the songs he remembered from his own school days. A little bit of light broke through the heaviness he'd been carrying around. He wanted to ignore the feeling, because he didn't want to attribute it to being around Sadie.

Levi didn't want another woman to work her way into his life. But the lightheartedness stayed with him as he dipped the paintbrush into the half-empty can. There was no denying the power of Sadie's positive attitude.

They worked until lunchtime.

"Come on, everyone. I believe you've more than earned a lunch break." Looking at Levi, Sadie said, "You, too, Levi. I know

I've worked up an appetite, and I don't care if that doesn't sound ladylike. I'm starving!"

He saw the flush of her cheeks that came with working hard in the summertime heat. With a laugh, Sadie spun on her heel and hurried out the door, stopping at the water pump to the right of the building to wash her hands.

"Boys, don't forget, cleanliness is next to godliness," she called out as Jeremiah, Mica and Josh plowed by her.

They turned around and rushed back to splash their hands in the water after she finished. Levi waited his turn, then putting his hands together, he splashed the water up on his face. The coolness refreshed him.

They formed a short line behind Sadie to get a hamburger hot off the grill that Jeremiah's *mudder* had set up.

"I thought you might be getting tired of the sandwiches. So, I had my husband bring over our gas grill."

"*Danke*, Susan." Sadie patted the woman on the forearm. "Your thoughtfulness is much appreciated."

"Danke," Levi added. The delicious scent of the burgers caused his stomach to rumble loud enough for Sadie to hear.

"We'd best get you fed, Levi. I don't need

you collapsing. And when you're ready, I want to talk to you about the new shed."

Levi blinked. They'd agreed to work together on the schoolhouse repair, and then he would be free to continue with the shed. The rebuild would be straightforward. A simple shed. Yes, he knew it was the school's shed, but they were on a tight schedule.

What could she possibly have to say about the shed project?

Chapter Seven

Sadie could tell by the look on Levi's face that he wasn't thrilled with her request. His mouth had taken on the same determined line she remembered from the day she'd first met him.

She pasted a smile on her face. Taking her paper plate with the hamburger and macaroni salad over to the picnic table, she joined the boys. After a few minutes, Levi sat at the opposite end of the bench.

It was clear he did not want to discuss the shed project over lunch. That was fine by her. She was content to enjoy every last bite of her hamburger. The boys sat across from them, inhaling their food.

"Boys. Slow down when you eat. I don't want you choking."

All three of them looked up at her, as if they'd forgotten their manners and that she and Levi were at the table with them.

"*Es dutt mir leed*, Miss Sadie," Jeremiah said. Nudging Josh with his right elbow, he added, "We're all sorry."

The other two boys put what was left of their burgers on the plate and nodded.

Leaning across the table, Jeremiah said, "My *mudder* makes the best burgers."

"*Danke*, son." Susan accepted the compliment as she joined them with her own plate. "Sadie, I cannot believe how much work you've gotten done in such a short time."

Sadie watched as the boys went back to eating at a much slower pace, then turned to Susan. "I've had a lot of help."

Susan glanced over to where Levi sat. "It was *gut* that you came along to our village when you did, Levi Byler. You've certainly been a great help to our Sadie and our school community. Though, I imagine your own community must miss you."

A look Sadie couldn't identify slid across Levi's face. Was it sadness or longing, maybe regret? She imagined he must be a bit homesick. Maybe not, though. It was hard to say, because she hadn't had any conversations with him about his life. She only knew the little that she'd learned the day he rescued her from the mudhole. And, of course, that blue was his favorite color.

They finished eating their lunch and returned to work. Levi got the boys set up painting the wall behind Sadie's desk while she continued to work on the trim around the windows. She was painting the lower half of the one by the entryway when Levi came up behind her with a brush in hand.

"I'll do the tops so you don't have to worry about standing on the ladder."

"That's very kind of you." Sadie grew pensive. Their close proximity brought her the perfect opportunity to learn more about him.

As she dipped her brush into their shared paint can, she formulated her questions. She enjoyed learning about people. One of her favorite classes to teach was history. For a few days she and the *kinder* got lost in learning about the people who had come and gone before them. She wondered again what Levi's people might be like.

"Tell me, Levi, what is your community like?"

His movements stilled. Sadie thought the question was innocent enough. She continued moving the brush up and down the trim in short strokes. Waiting.

"I live closer to the city than you do. But we have farmland and ten church districts," he said. "Some are smaller than others."

"And your family?"

"My family?"

"Do you have a large family? I know you're part of Jacob's family, but what is your immediate family like? Most of us around here have large families, and some live near their elders or in the same house if it's big enough. My friend Lizzie's sister lives in the house they grew up in, with her husband and *kinder.* Lizzie and her husband, Paul, moved into the village to be closer to their shop."

"I see. I have two older *bruders* and a younger sister. They are all married off."

"But you're not." Sadie drew in a breath, surprised when she voiced her thought. "*Es dutt mir leed.* That is none of my business."

Levi turned away from her, appearing to concentrate on touching up the paint on the windows. Then he said, "I understand. We're at a time in our lives when courtships are all our families want to talk about."

"Perhaps I spend too much time ruminating about the subject." Softly she added, "I know you overheard my conversation with Lizzie."

"Ah. *Ja.* I might have heard some of what you were saying." He raised an eyebrow, studying her.

A shiver ran along her spine. It wasn't an unwanted feeling. Still, Sadie found herself wondering at her reaction to Levi. She was about to tell him she'd no interest in the man her *vader* wanted for her, then changed her mind. She didn't think Levi would care to hear her thoughts on the matter.

Eventually she turned away from him, focusing on her work. The only sound in the room came from the movement of the brushes and rollers. Even the boys had settled into a rhythm. Sweat trickled down Sadie's back, and she longed for a wisp of a breeze to come through the open windows. All the while she wished she could take back her words about Levi's marital state. His family and his life before coming here were none of her business.

They continued working in silence until she looked up and realized the room was finished.

Sadie sent the boys home, leaving her and Levi to finish the cleanup. She was helping him fold the drop cloth when he finally started talking to her again.

"What are your thoughts on the shed?" he asked, taking her side of the folded cloth out of her hands.

Clearing her throat, she knew her idea might sound like extra work. "I want to add in two windows in the front so we can use them to start our seedlings for the garden. And I think some window boxes would be nice, too. This way the students can try out different types of plants."

"You have windows here." He pointed to the ones they'd just painted.

"We do, but they don't get the right light to grow seedlings in."

"It seems to be bright enough now."

"Yes, but this is the summer sunlight. The early-spring light comes in from that direction." Sadie nodded toward the east side of the room.

"And you can't use those windows?"

"*Nee.* The sills are not wide enough." She saw the stubborn set of his jaw and put her hands on her hips.

She would fight to the end for her students, and even though this might seem unimportant to him, for her this little thing was worth the effort.

Levi stared at her. She waited for his gaze to waver, and when it didn't, she broke the stare down by casting her gaze to the toes of her shoes. That was when she saw the paint spatters and knew her *mamm* would not be happy with her for making a mess of them yet again.

"Doesn't Jacob have a shed that we can use here?" she finally asked. "One with windows?"

"*Nee.* We're going to build this one on-site. He's swamped with business. Even before the storm, his orders were backed up, and now with people needing theirs replaced, he's running out of stock."

She nibbled on her lip, trying to come up with a way to convince Levi to add the windows to the new shed. "Is it the cost?"

"Nope."

"So, it's you not wanting to change your plans?"

"I guess it's been a long day and I don't have the energy left to think about changing any existing plans," he admitted to her.

Stubbing her toe along the floorboard, she

grumbled, "I understand. But don't you think my idea is a *gut* one?"

"I do. However, it's not really up to us to make these changes."

She pondered his words, knowing the school board had put Jacob in charge of this project. He was a trusted member of the community. Surely, he would do this for her.

"What I want is to have an area for my students to work on their gardening skills."

Levi took the drop cloth over to the pile of leftover supplies. He fumbled around for a few minutes, tapping a hammer on top of the loosened paint can lid. Then he picked up the can and the drop cloth, brushing past her, and carried them out the front door.

Sadie hurried after him. Her patience thinning, and knowing the fatigue might be fueling her, she called out to him, "Levi! We're not finished with this."

He set the supplies in the back of his wagon. She saw the sweat breaking through the back of his shirt and knew he had to be as tired and worn out by the heat as she was. But that didn't stop her from wanting to know if he might at least consider her suggestions for the windows.

Resting an elbow on the side of the wagon,

Levi pushed the brim of his straw hat off his forehead. Sadie tipped her head back a bit, looking up into his eyes. The blue-green color was striking in the afternoon light.

She ignored that thought, even though she knew many of her friends would consider him to be a handsome man. And she wouldn't be able to contradict them on that observation.

Her nerves became a jangle, a feeling she wasn't familiar with. Normally, she would plow through to make her point. But standing here, at the end of a long day spent working side by side, Sadie felt her conviction about the windows waver.

Nee. She must stop thinking like a schoolgirl and remember the interests of her students.

Using a soft, relenting tone, she asked, "Levi, will you please help me out here?"

He knew what she was doing, and while he might not trust her cajoling tone, he understood why she wanted him to make the changes. He supposed there wasn't any harm in bringing her idea to Jacob. She was right about one thing: the students' needs should come first.

Finally, he said, "I'll talk to Jacob."

He went back inside and brought out the rest of the cans, brushes and rollers. Sadie helped him clean up, until the exhaustion of the day caught up with her. Levi noticed her steps slowing on the last trip to the wagon. In two easy strides, he came alongside her, taking the can.

"Danke," she said, releasing the metal handle.

He squinted down at her, "Sadie, you've done a good day's work here. Let me drive you home."

"That won't be necessary. I rode my bike over this morning."

"Come on, it's too hot to ride it back home. The wagon will take half the time. I can put the bike in the back."

He saw her indecision, as well as her flushed cheeks. She had to be feeling the heat as much as he was.

She narrowed her eyes, as if she had a choice in the matter. "I don't want you to get any ideas about my needing rescuing, like the first time we met."

Biting back a half smile, he replied, "Nope. Think of it as a neighbor helping out a neighbor."

"All right. I left my bike near the pop-up canopy. Would you mind getting it for me?"

"I can do that."

After finding her bike, he wheeled it back and loaded it on the wagon. Then he offered her his hand, which surprisingly she took hold of. If he'd learned one thing about Sadie Fischer in his short time here, it was that she had an independent streak. Levi waited for her to settle in the seat, and then going around to the other side, he climbed in, as well. The wagon shifted under his weight and caused Sadie to bump into him.

She pulled away from him with a soft "I'm sorry."

Once back on her side of the seat, Sadie continued, "I guess I am more tired than I thought I was. You know how you go and go and go and then when you stop, you realize how much energy you've spent? That's how I'm feeling."

Urging the horse forward, Levi nodded. He did know. Right now, his shoulders and arms ached from all the painting. Sadie had to be feeling the same discomfort and yet she sat with her back tall and her hands folded neatly on her lap, looking out over the passing hills. Meanwhile, the blister on his right hand was still bothering him. He'd have to be sure to clean and bandage it when he got back to Jacob and Rachel's place.

"Levi, before I forget. We have our annual Miller's Crossing picnic coming up. You must be sure to come. You'll be able to meet more of our community. A lot of the older folks don't come out except for our gatherings, and of course the weekly church services. There will be lots of food and games," she went on. "I might even find time to make my blue-ribbon snickerdoodles! My *mamm* will, of course, make her potato salad, and there will be coleslaw and moon pies. I'm sure there will be a roasted chicken and bratwurst."

She groaned in delight. "My *grossmudder*, on my *vader*'s side, made the best bratwurst. She passed over a decade ago, but we still use her recipe at large gatherings." She rubbed a hand over her stomach. "All of this talk about food is making me hungry. Trust me, the day of the picnic will be filled with fun, and it's a *gut* time to catch up. Which reminds me, you never finished telling me about your people." She gave him a smile.

He knew she was trying to find out what brought him here. And he wasn't willing to share his personal life with her. Sadie didn't need to know about his past. He certainly didn't want her to get any ideas about adding him to her list of what she wanted for her perfect Amish man. He was anything but perfect.

He thought back on this time last year when his life had seemed cemented in place.

He'd been working with his *vader* on the family farm. Because Levi had always been good with the craftsman side of things, he'd been in charge of all the building upkeep. And he'd been in love with a young woman he'd known all his life. Levi thought Anne had been a perfect match. She was kind and gentle. When their families proposed the idea of their courtship, it had seemed like the most natural path for them.

They'd made plans for their wedding day, after which they were going to live in a small house near the back of Levi's family farm. He'd spent weeks cleaning and painting, inside and out. Because he knew how much Anne liked to work on her quilting, he'd set up a separate space off to one side of the living room for her to work in. He'd built a shelf along one wall with cubbies for all her fabric.

Levi had intended those white shelves to be her wedding gift. The only problem was Anne had had other plans. While Levi had been planning a life with the woman he loved, she'd been plotting to leave their community. Absently, he rubbed his hand over his chest, knowing nothing could remove the remnants of the dull ache that still lay inside his heart.

The day he realized Anne had gone still stood out in his memories. His plan on the beautiful sunny fall day had been to put the finishing touches on the house. But when he'd gotten there, he'd found a note taped to the front door. Her words seared into his soul. She was in love with someone else: an *Englischer*. Under the cover of darkness, Anne had left the community.

And in the blink of an eye his life changed.

For days afterward he found himself falling into a well of sadness he didn't think would ever end. Then came the anger. Anger at himself for believing in something that would never be. Anger at Anne for her deception.

Questioning his every move since the day they'd agreed to the courtship, he let his work on the farm go. He spent hours in prayer seeking an answer from the Lord and realizing there might not be one. Until one day his *mudder* came to him with the letter from his cousin. She was the one who convinced him to come here, telling him he needed a new outlook on life. And reminding him that the Lord never gave anyone more than they could handle.

Pausing in his thoughts, he brought his attention back to Sadie. He pushed down all those memories, all those thoughts and feelings, and gave a shrug. "There's not much more to tell."

"Do you miss them?"

He'd have to add *tenacious* to the list of words that described the schoolteacher.

"I've sent them off a letter or two. My *mamm* is *gut* about responding with news. Besides, I'm not sure if this will be a permanent move for me." Levi paused. He had no idea why he'd voiced that thought.

"Right, because you're here to help out your cousin. Who knows, Levi. Miller's Crossing might grow on you and maybe you'll never want to leave."

Her voice drifted off, leaving only the sound of nature and the occasional car zipping by them. Sadie seemed satisfied with their conversation, for now. This young woman was a force to be reckoned with. He'd seen how patient and kind she was with the lads helping them out. And she always, always had a smile for everyone. Levi could tell from the way she took care of the things in her classroom that she was a devoted teacher.

Though he had to admit, he couldn't imagine her scolding anyone, let alone a *kinder*. And her stubbornness? Even that had a soft side.

He knew he shouldn't be thinking this way. He'd learned a hard lesson this past year about trusting his feelings when it came to love. But even in this short amount of time, Sadie Fischer had worked her way into his thoughts. He would be better served focusing his attention on his work with Jacob.

Levi looked out over the landscape unfolding before them. Rolling hills and trees filled with lush green leaves lay on the tapestry the Lord had created. The air, though heavy with the summer humidity, was pure and clean. The rhythmic sound of the horse's hooves tapping along the road settled over him. Levi's mind wandered.

He imagined life here in Miller's Crossing, though tough at times, could in turn be filled with grace and beauty. The people he'd met so far were kind and caring. The nearby village of Clymer had buildings that were obviously cared for with pride. Levi didn't know where life was going to take him. He only knew to trust in the path laid out before him…the path that had brought him here. Still, he couldn't help battling with the changes in his life. He knew for certain he would use caution when it came to making decisions that would last a lifetime.

He suspected that the others, like Sadie, didn't know what to make of him, but like all Amish communities, they were welcoming. And the fact that he had family here helped. He felt he was doing good work at the school, which led him to an idea. One that might make Sadie's workload easier. And even as he had the thought, Levi knew he was going down an emotional path that he shouldn't be taking.

He still believed his life was meant to be lived alone. But that didn't mean he couldn't do something helpful for Sadie. After he dropped her off at her house, he'd take advantage of the lingering summer daylight and head back to the school.

Glancing to his right, he realized Sadie hadn't spoken in quite a few minutes. Her chin was tipped down, and he could see the even rise and fall of her chest. Her hands, though still together, lay limp in her lap.

"Well, I'll be," he muttered in amusement. She'd fallen asleep.

Laying a light hand against her forearm, he gave her the tiniest of shakes. "Sadie. Sadie. Wake up."

Chapter Eight

Sadie sat up with a start, blinking. She'd fallen asleep. How had she let that happen? She must have been more tired than she thought. Embarrassment flooded through her. How could she let herself be caught in such a compromising position? She worked at brushing the wrinkles out of her apron.

"I wasn't sleeping. I was simply resting my eyes." She couldn't believe she'd resorted to using one of her *grossmudder* Fischer's responses when caught napping.

"If you say so."

Sitting up taller, she quipped, "I do."

By now, Levi was guiding the horse and wagon around the last bend before her home. She could tell by the slant of the sun that it was nearly past suppertime.

"Oh, dear."

"What's the matter?" Levi asked.

"I'm late for dinner."

"We should have left the school sooner."

"But we were busy with painting. My *mamm* will understand my tardiness."

Her *vader*, on the other hand, might not be as accommodating. He liked to have everyone at the table at the same time each evening. Sadie often wondered how he could be so strict with his routine, while she liked to see how the day would unfold. She liked to think that was what made her a better schoolteacher. While she did use a lesson planner that the committee approved each semester, she also set aside time just in case an educational opportunity arose that needed further exploration.

Take last spring when the girls had wanted to know more about the painting Lizzie Burkholder did. Lizzie was getting quite the reputation for her watercolor landscapes. Sadie had spent a week on art, giving a little time each day to let the students dabble in the paints. Indeed, schooling should be used to teach the fundamentals, but Sadie would never subdue her students' natural curiosity. They were young for such a short time, and the adult world would be upon them soon enough.

And that thought brought her full circle to her *vader*'s concerns that she needed to concentrate more on her future beyond the classroom. Her gaze slid to Levi. He seemed intent on steering the wagon around the corner and down her driveway.

She wondered again why he hadn't brought a wife with him to Miller's Crossing. He seemed reluctant to discuss his family when she'd asked. While some might think a man like Levi wasn't the marrying kind, Sadie could tell he cared. Even though he was quiet and pensive, he'd been helpful to her these past days. When they were working at the school, she'd caught him watching over the boys, teaching them how to do things the right way. And he'd worked tirelessly alongside her.

The wagon came to a stop near the hitching post at the front of the house. Sadie hopped down. The first thing she noticed was that the barn had been closed up for the night. And the picnic table in the side yard had been set with the plastic red-and-white-checkered tablecloth. Her *mamm* and sister were busy setting out the food.

Sara looked up when she saw Sadie and Levi. Giving them a wave, she beckoned them over.

"Come. You're just in time. *Mamm* and I were just putting dinner out," Sara said. Taking the lid off of the beef stew, she added, "Our *bruder* William and Kara are coming over with their *kinder*. They should be here any minute."

As if on cue, Sadie heard the laughter of her niece and nephew. She turned to watch as William parked the buggy next to Levi's wagon. William and his family lived about a mile up the road at his wife's family home. Sadie was happy to see them.

"Kara! William! *Guten owed*." Sadie greeted them, giving the *kinder* a big hug.

"*Guten owed* to you, Sadie," her *bruder* said with a nod. He looked to where Levi was getting her bike out of the back of the wagon. "And who might this be?" he asked.

"This is Levi Byler. He's been helping out with the school repairs."

"*Ach*. That was a fierce storm." William held out his hand and Levi shook it.

Sadie looked back and forth between the two men. Her *bruder* was a clever one. Acting nice and neighborly when she knew he was, in fact, taking stock of the man.

"*Ja*, it was indeed," she agreed. "But we're moving along. Tomorrow I have to go to King's Stationery to replace the school supplies that were ruined."

She walked with Kara and the *kinder* while William stayed back to chat with Levi.

"I'm not sure your *bruder* is too happy to see you with that man," Kara commented.

Sadie made a face. Though she loved him dearly, and he was the eldest, William was not in charge of her life. "Levi offered to bring me home. We had a long day's work. I have to admit I was too tired to pedal all the way here. I appreciated the ride."

Sara met them halfway to the picnic table. "*Mamm* wants to know if Levi might like to join us for supper."

The suggestion caught Sadie off guard. It hadn't occurred to her to ask Levi to stay. She knew he had to get back to Jacob's, and that was at least a twenty-minute drive from here. She imagined he would say no. However, she didn't get the chance to invite him. William came over a few minutes later as Levi was driving off.

"He seems nice enough," was all William said.

Sadie nodded, thinking that Levi was indeed nice enough. Her gaze lingered on the roadway as she watched the wagon disappear over the horizon.

"Sadie, come, dinner is waiting to be served."

Sadie smiled at her *mamm* and approached the table. A large maple tree spread shade over the area, and she took a moment to drink in the scene. Her parents, two of her siblings, and the *kinder* all took their places on the wooden benches. She sat between her *mamm* and sister and joined in the thanksgiving for the food set before them.

The breeze floated around them, offering the first bit of coolness she'd felt all day. She wanted to tip her head back and take in the moment, but she tamped down the urge, instead spooning some of the stew onto her plate.

"How far have you gotten at the school?" Sara asked, handing Sadie the bread basket.

"I have a few more days before I can begin to bring in the desks and bookshelves. Tomorrow I'm going to the stationery store to get some supplies."

"William can take you. He has to run there himself," Kara offered. William and Kara ran a small quilt shop out of their home.

From the far end of the table, William said, "I'll pick you up at eight."

Sadie agreed, then finished the meal and helped with the evening chores.

The next morning, she was ready when William pulled into the driveway at eight on the dot. She settled into the buggy and bade him a *guder mariye*.

"I hope your morning is a *gut* one, too, Sadie," he returned.

She'd say it was. The humidity that had been plaguing them for the past week had finally broken overnight, leaving in its wake a clear blue sky and easy breathing. She glanced at her *bruder*—from this side, he reminded her a lot of their *vader*. Both men had the same long nose and graying beards, though her *vader*'s was almost all white now. William had the same shape to his eyes, although the color resembled their *mudder*'s.

He gave the reins a shake and the horse trotted off. Sadie sat back under the cover of the buggy.

"Sadie, I'm not going to waste any time. I need to speak with you about your situation."

She felt the tiny hairs on the back of her neck rise. This couldn't be good. "And what situation might that be?"

"This one between you and Isaiah."

She tried to keep her frustration in check. "As I've told our *vader*, there is no situation there."

"You know there should be."

"I know no such thing, William." She felt her anger rising.

Annoyance didn't do anyone any good. But now she had a feeling that William bringing her into the village hadn't been a kind offer. He'd been wanting to find a way to speak to her about her future, and a ride into the village was a good excuse. Sadie looked out the small window of the buggy. The horse moved along at such a speed that the trees and hillside whizzed by them.

"William, slow down!" She felt the buggy slowing. *"Danke."*

He mumbled, *"Es dutt mir leed."* A mere second passed and then he continued, "Sadie, you are the schoolteacher and as such you have to live up to a certain standard."

"William! Are you saying you think that I'm not good enough for the job?" Sadie felt flushed. She couldn't accept that her *bruder* would think such a thing of his own sister. She worked night and day during the school year planning and preparing for her students to get the best education they could under her tutelage.

"*Nee. Nee.* Of course not. But you have been ignoring *Vader*'s choice for you, and people are beginning to take notice."

"I don't care."

"You should care!"

"Don't raise your voice to me."

William let out an exasperated sigh. "Oh, Sadie. We, and by we, I mean our family, only want what is best for you."

"Maybe what's best for me would be for you to let me make my own choice in this matter."

"I don't want to see this cause you any trouble."

"See what causing me trouble, William?"

"Your being with Levi Byler. He's driven you home, not once but twice. And you are spending time working with him at the schoolhouse."

"For goodness' sake. Neither of those times count for anything. The first time he rescued me from that mudhole, and yesterday he was doing nothing more than being a good neighbor." Sucking in a breath, she breathed out, "As for being alone at the school, there are others there most of the time."

"*Most* of the time, but not all of the time," William pointed out.

By now they had traveled to the outskirts of Miller's Crossing. The stationery store was over the next rise and then a turn down a narrow, winding road. Sadie grabbed onto the handrail as William allowed the buggy to sail around the corner. Taking his anger out on the poor horse wouldn't help the matter.

"Slow down," she said once more. "Did *Vader* ask you to speak to me?"

"*Nee*. He did not. I'm the one who is concerned." William's voice softened as he slowed the horse coming into the parking lot for King's Stationery. He pulled into a space, tugging the brake back and setting it. Then he turned to look at her.

"Levi Byler seems like a nice person. And yes, helping you with the repairs is a *gut* thing. But you are the teacher. You know you have to be careful with your time and you shouldn't be unchaperoned. Just be careful. Okay?"

Sadie could see that concern softening the edges around his eyes and knew he only had her best interest at heart. She didn't like arguing and hated that they were starting this glorious day sparring over her future.

"Sadie, please consider my words."

"I will."

They entered the store. William headed off to the office supply section, and Sadie went to the aisle that had the classroom materials. It didn't take her long to find the two posters she needed, then she made a beeline to the books. She hoped they had a replacement for a title that had been destroyed by the rain.

She slowed her pace, enjoying the covers on display. An entire row was filled with Christian books with such beautiful art that Sadie paused to admire them. Then she saw a few gardening magazines and the *Farmers' Almanac*. Finally, she found the children's section and was delighted to see the book she'd been looking for. She added it to her basket, then she went up to the front counter to pay for everything.

Her *bruder* had gotten there ahead of her and was chatting with Amos King, the owner of the store and one of the school board members.

"*Gute mariye*, Miss Sadie."

"It's a fine morning, Amos. I think we're in for the best day of the week so far."

"I would agree." He smiled at her and then

slid the book into a paper bag. "Should I add these to the school account?"

"Yes, please."

"My *kinder* are anxious to start the new school year. They were very upset to see the storm damage. But I assured them it would be taken care of in plenty of time."

"I've had a lot of *gut* people helping. Some of the older boys have been working inside with me on the painting."

"So I've heard." And as if to prove William's point, Amos added, "Jacob's cousin Levi has done *gut* work there. But please be sure to work in groups."

Sadie turned her back ever so slightly so she didn't have to see the look on her *bruder*'s face. She hated to admit when he was right. It was clear that the community members were indeed talking about her. Sadie didn't want to create any problems for the school board when it came to her personal life.

Sadie chastised herself. She knew better. She needed to give more thought to her actions.

Nodding at Amos, she gathered her things and headed out to the buggy. William came right on her heels. Thankfully he had the wherewithal to keep his comments to himself regarding what Amos had said.

William dropped her at the school, and Sadie thanked him for taking her to the store. "I appreciate the ride, William."

"It's no trouble. You'll think about what I said?"

"Ja."

Sadie waved him off, knowing that where Isaiah Troyer was concerned her mind was made up.

She walked along the pathway to the front door. She swung it open, fully expecting to find the blue tape surrounding the windows and floor trim. But that wasn't what she found at all.

Sadie stood in the middle of the room with her mouth agape.

"I don't understand," she whispered in amazement at the sight before her.

Chapter Nine

Sadie set the posters and book down on the desk. The desk right in front of her. The room was full of them! She spun around with her arms spread wide in happiness.

All the desks were in orderly rows, and the bookcases were set up against the wall near the door. Her teacher's desk was still absent, but that didn't matter. She wondered who she should thank for this gift.

The sound of voices came from behind the building. Sadie hurried out the door and ran around to the back, anxious to see who was there.

Levi stood with Jacob and two of the boys who'd been helping her out.

"Danke!" she blurted out. *"Danke! Danke!"*

"Miss Sadie, were you surprised?" Mica asked.

"I was very pleasantly surprised. *Danke* so much."

"It was Levi's idea. He'd already gotten the cleanup done. All the desks were set out. Josh and I helped bring up the bookshelves this morning."

"Well, that was very kind of all of you." Sadie nodded to each of the boys and then raised her eyes to meet Levi's gaze.

His expression was unreadable She wondered when he'd found the time to do all of this work. It had been quite late in the day when he'd left her house yesterday and it was only midmorning now.

"Levi, I can't believe you found the time to do all of this!"

He was half turned away from her, as if he didn't want to meet her gaze. "I came back last night."

"You didn't have to do this," she said. His generosity touched her.

"I thought getting the desks back up here would push us along. Now you can concentrate on getting the classroom ready for opening day."

There seemed to be a different mood about

him this morning. She couldn't quite put her finger on the change. But it was as if he didn't want to be near her. Sadie didn't understand. Maybe Levi was distracted thinking about the tasks for today. Either way, she was grateful for his effort.

"*Danke* again for your thoughtfulness."

While she'd been offering her thanks, two wagonloads of lumber arrived, one with two-by-fours and the other with roof trusses. Sadie watched as the drivers pulled to a stop next to the old shed foundation.

Levi still hadn't agreed to add in windows. Deciding she could catch more bees with honey, Sadie flashed him her most radiant smile. She needed him to fix the shed the way it should be done. *For the children, of course.*

Not wanting to be in the way, Sadie left the men to carry on.

After seeing the look on Sadie's face when she'd come around back, he thought his late night, working by the light of one of the most brilliant moons he'd seen in a long time, had been worth it. After he'd dropped her at home, he'd come back to the school and finished taking down the tape, swept the floor, cleaned up a few cobwebs and hauled thirty desks up the flight of basement stairs.

Ja, he'd been exhausted, but it was *gut* exhaustion, the kind that came when you knew you'd done something that would make someone else happy. Sadie had been so tired at the end of yesterday, and while he knew she would work without complaint, he wanted to do something that would make today easier.

He hadn't meant to sound terse with his response just now, but Levi knew from hard experience that Sadie's feelings were softening toward him. The tells were there. The way she spoke to him with a lighter tone, the way her gaze grew steady when she looked at him. He knew the signs because those were the exact emotions he'd experienced with Anne.

Levi wasn't about to be taken in again. He had to be careful where Sadie was concerned, because she was beginning to grow on him.

"Levi!"

He turned to see Jacob coming toward him.

"I'm going to unload these wagons and then we'll be back with the rest of the lumber you'll need to get started on the shed."

"Okay. What were your thoughts on adding in the windows that Sadie asked for?"

"I still have to see if we have any in stock.

I might have two older ones we could use. But go ahead and start with the framework as we originally planned. I don't want to have to redo the walls if we don't have those windows."

"That sounds like a *gut* plan."

Jacob gave him a wink, joking, "Do you want me to tell Sadie?"

"*Nee*. We won't say anything until we know for certain."

"All right then. On second thought, I'm going to send one of my workers back with the next load. I still have a month's backlog to deal with. I'm thankful you came out to Miller's Crossing when you did. I'm not sure how I could have been in all these places at once."

"I'm happy to help."

"You're more than helping, Levi. We'll talk more about the business when things settle down. Have a good day."

"You, too," Levi replied.

Watching his friend leave, he wondered what Jacob had meant. He heard the boys laughing behind him. Turning around, he found Mica and Josh horsing around on the pile of two-by-fours. They were pushing and shoving each other on and off the pile.

"Boys! Get down from there before you

get hurt!" Levi didn't like to raise his voice, but he didn't have time to tend to an injury. "Come here."

Doing as they were told, the two of them scrambled over to him.

Folding his arms, Levi stared down at them.

Mica fidgeted in front of him. "We didn't mean no harm, Levi," he said.

"I understand. But we've got a lot of work to do today. Do either of you boys know anything about putting up a shed?"

"Nope," Josh said.

"How old are you?"

"I'm twelve and Mica is eleven," Josh answered.

Raising an eyebrow, Levi asked, "Do you know how to swing a hammer?"

Both boys nodded.

"*Gut.* Then let's get to work." Of course, Levi had no intention of letting the boys work with hammers and nails. He just wanted them to concentrate on helping him and not roughhousing.

They'd done well enough with the painting, but working with lumber required focus.

"I'm going to tell you what I need help with, and you let me know if you think you can handle it." Levi took an authoritative stance with his feet spread apart and his arms folded across his chest while he let his words sink in.

After a few seconds, both boys stilled.

"I'll need help carrying the wood over to the foundation, then I'll need someone to hold the pieces in place while I nail them in position. You think you can do that?"

Both boys nodded so hard their hats tumbled off their blond heads.

Clapping his hands together, Levi said, "Okay then, put your hats back on and let's get a move on."

For the next few hours, Levi had to delve deep for patience. Mica and Josh took turns holding the two-by-fours while he pounded the nails in place. Though they were good helpers, they would wander off when he wasn't watching them like a hawk.

He didn't understand their behavior. Yesterday they'd been diligent while working with Sadie. Today they were acting like little *kinder*. Listening to them horsing around reminded him of his own childhood with his *bruders*. They'd managed to get into their fair share of trouble during chore time.

Putting the hammer back into the leather

work belt he wore around his waist, Levi tilted his hat and wiped his brow with his sleeve. Blowing out a breath, he surveyed the work they'd done. It might be a good idea to nail the frame of the walls together on the ground and then push them up into place. For that he'd need the strength of a few men. Not as many as a barn raising required; just two would suffice.

He thought the boys might be happy to hear they wouldn't be needed for that part.

"Mica, Josh!" he called to them. "Come on over here. You've earned a break."

"Are you pleased with our work today, Levi?" Josh wanted to know.

"I am. You've done a fine job. Now, here's the thing, and I know you'll be disappointed, but I'm not going to need you for a few days. I'm bringing some men in to help me with the wall frames. It's a big job."

The boys did their best to look solemn, but then their faces broke out in grins. Saying their goodbyes, they bounded off across the schoolyard.

"Well, I'll be." Levi shook his head and laughed.

Some days he missed the freedom of being a young boy. The long summers spent fishing and playing in the hayloft. The time before the responsibilities of life intruded.

As Levi laughed to himself, he noticed Sadie coming around the back, picking her way through the construction debris.

"It looks like they were itching to leave you." Her comment came out in a chuckle.

He liked her laugh.

"They hung on longer than I thought they would. Let's face it, working with you inside is nothing like being out here helping lift heavy lumber. But they are *gut* boys."

"*Ja.* They are." Walking over to the pile of two-by-fours, she looked down at them. "I don't see any windows."

"Now, Sadie, before you go getting all in a huff, Jacob is going to look around to see what he has in stock."

Though she tried to hide it, Levi saw the satisfied smile cross her face. "That's very nice of him, and of you, to take my request seriously."

It was more that he didn't want to get bogged down arguing with her over the matter when there was so much work yet to be done.

She stood there with a look he couldn't quite figure out. Her eyes were scrunched up a bit as if she were deep in thought. He fiddled with the hammer stuck in his tool belt.

Finally, she said, "You're good with the *kinder*, Levi."

A jolt of surprise ran through him. He hadn't expected her compliment. With a shrug, he said, "I like them well enough."

"I can tell. It's hard to be patient when all they want to do is be allowed to run free. But you took your time with Mica and Josh today. That was nice of you."

"Danke."

She grinned up at him. "Like it or not, Levi, you are becoming a part of this community."

He didn't say anything. He still wasn't sure he'd be staying on here. But he did like the people, and they were friendly toward him. He was aware of how Sadie's *vader* and oldest *bruder* felt about him. Not that it mattered. Levi was not in the market to find a wife.

"Do you work on projects like this with the *kinder* in your family?"

"If the need arises."

He knew this young woman well enough to know she was trying to bait him into sharing more of his past with her. No matter how sweet she tried to be, Levi couldn't let himself fall into her trap.

"Sadie, I really need to get back to work."

"I'll let you go, but promise me you'll come to the picnic."

Chapter Ten

A week later, Sadie stood in the kitchen putting the finishing touches on the final batch of her blue-ribbon snickerdoodles and thinking about her last exchange with Levi. While she rolled the dough into one-inch balls and dropped them into a bowl of cinnamon and sugar, she realized he'd never given her an answer about whether or not he would be attending today's picnic.

Using a spoon, she coated the unbaked dough with the mixture. She'd gotten out of bed right before sunrise to avoid running the oven in the heat of the day. The entire house smelled like vanilla, cinnamon and warm sugar. Oh, how she loved the scent. Inhaling, she let the smells flood her senses with homey goodness and comfort.

It had been a busy month, but she was looking forward to the annual Miller's Crossing picnic. The day was much like a wedding celebration, but in her mind even better, because you didn't have to wear your Sunday clothes. Today was a day to celebrate life, community and friendships. And Sadie couldn't wait to catch up with her friends.

Setting the balls of dough on the tray, being careful to leave two inches between each one for spreading, she put them in the oven to bake.

She grabbed the chicken-shaped timer off the Formica countertop, setting it for eight minutes. While the cookies were baking, she had two other sheet pans cooling with a few dozen snickerdoodles. The sight of their crackled tops brought a smile to her face.

Sliding a flat spatula under each cookie, she carefully transferred them to a wire rack where they would finish hardening. Later, she would put them in a big red cookie tin. If anyone asked her what her favorite thing to do was other than teaching, she'd have to say baking these cookies. How could you not love a good old-fashioned cookie?

She wondered what Levi's favorite cookie might be. She remembered mentioning her snickerdoodles to him the day he'd brought her home from school. The same day her *bruder* had spoken to him.

Sadie didn't understand why her family couldn't leave her to make her own decision when it came to finding the right person to spend the rest of her life with.

Isaiah hadn't been around much at all. Come to think of it, she hadn't seen him since that day he'd stopped by to see the storm damage at the school. The day Levi had interrupted their conversation. She'd known he wanted to know who Isaiah was. But they didn't discuss those matters. Instead their conversations stayed focused on the school or the little bits when she could get him to talk about his family.

Sadie had tried on more than one occasion to get Levi to open up about his life. In her opinion, he was very good at keeping his life closed. She didn't know why this bothered her so much. His behavior toward her had continued to be polite, but still she found herself wanting to get to know him better.

The spatula fell from her hand, landing on the floor with a clatter.

She liked Levi Byler.

"Oh, dear."

"Sadie, what on earth is all the noise about?" her *mamm* asked, rushing into the kitchen to shut off the timer.

Sadie had been so lost in her thoughts that she hadn't even heard the timer buzzing.

"And who are you talking to?"

"No one." Giving her head a shake, she admitted, "Myself." She picked up the spatula, walked to the sink and rinsed it off.

"Well, your distraction almost caused your cookies to burn." Her *mamm* grabbed a pot holder off a nearby hook, opened the oven and slid the tray out, setting it on top of the stove. "Your *vader* should be in from the barn soon. He wants to get over to the picnic early. Remember last year when one of his prized cows had all that trouble with her twisted stomach?"

She sure did remember. They were two hours late to the fun because they had to help chase the cow around in hopes of getting the poor beast's insides to right. The entire family was out running around in the pasture behind the barn. Eventually the cow settled down. This year the day looked brighter and worry-free.

While she waited for the cookies to cool, Sadie cleaned up her work area. She put the ingredients back in their place, wiped the countertop clean and then washed up the bowls and utensils. Meanwhile, her *mamm* put the finishing touches on her potato salad.

Sara came into the kitchen carrying the wicker picnic basket. She looked extra pretty today. Sadie wondered who her sister had in mind when she'd chosen to wear her best skirts.

"It's looking like we'll have perfect weather for the picnic," her sister observed.

"*Ja.* The sky is blue with only fair-weather clouds. Did you find the bread I set out in the pantry last night?" *Mamm* asked.

"I did. I already put the loaf in the basket along with a pound of butter."

"*Gut.* I think that will be plenty. And did you get out the sacks like I asked?"

"I did," Sara replied, wrinkling her nose. "I'm not going to participate in the sack race this year, so don't sign me up."

"*Ach*, me neither," Sadie agreed with her sister.

"Your school *kinder* will be disappointed if you don't join them, Sadie. You know that's a favorite at the picnic."

Taking the lid off the cookie tin, Sadie started layering the snickerdoodles inside.

"My *kinder* will be happy with me cheering them on from the sidelines, *Mamm*."

"If you say so."

"I'm bringing kites for them to fly."

"I guess they'll like that, too." Her *mamm* made a silly face at her.

Sadie laughed.

The potato salad and cookies, along with ice packs, were put inside the picnic basket. The bread was carefully placed on top, so as not to be crushed. Added to the mix were their paper plates and eating utensils. They didn't need to worry about the drinks because the Schrader family had a special wagon they loaned out for weddings that held half a dozen five-gallon containers of lemonade, iced tea and water. Perfect for an event such as this.

Sadie could feel the excitement building. This day was so much fun and she looked forward to it every year. It was a time for the farmers to take a much-needed break. And it was the last hurrah for the *kinder* before the start of the new school year. Maybe Levi had decided to join in the festivities.

"Come, come! Your *vader* is outside with the buggy." *Mamm* thrust the picnic hamper into Sadie's arms, ushering both her and Sara out the door.

"You sure are in a hurry, *Mamm*," Sara observed.

"I don't want to waste a minute of this day."

They all piled into the buggy, and by the time they reached the glade where the picnic had been set up, Sadie could see they were not the only ones with the idea of arriving early. The edge of the field had filled with wagons and buggies. There were *kinder* running about, and *mamms* and *vaders* hauling baskets and blankets over to where a long row of tables and benches had been set up.

Sadie saw Lizzie and Paul, with Rachel and Jacob behind them. Sadie waved. Then her heart thudded inside her chest as she spotted Levi carrying several tins in his hands.

He'd decided to join them.

Trying not to appear excited by his presence, Sadie meandered over to the table where her parents were unpacking. She helped her *mamm* set their places and then took her tin over to the dessert table, three lengths long and already filled with cobblers, pies and cakes. *What a sight to behold.* Their community was blessed with so many wonderful bakers and cooks. The neighboring tables held a variety of salads. Sadie's mouth watered.

She felt the breeze ruffle her blouse, and

then something light brushed against her back. She turned around to find Rachel standing behind her. Levi stood next to her, carrying the tins she'd seen him with a few minutes ago.

"Rachel. Levi. *Gute mariye.*" Sadie didn't know why it was happening, but she couldn't stop the heated flush of her cheeks. Her reaction to seeing Levi today was so schoolgirl. Quickly she busied herself taking the tin from his hands and setting it next to hers on the table.

"I recognize that tin." Rachel's voice penetrated the haze of Sadie's mind. "Did you make those blue-ribbon cookies?"

"I did."

"You are in for a real treat, Levi." Rachel nodded to him.

Levi stood there, shifting from one foot to the other, his gaze not quite meeting hers.

She wondered why, after all the time they'd just spent working on the school, that he suddenly seemed shy around her.

"Are you signing up for any of the events?" Rachel asked.

Sadie turned her attention to Rachel. "*Nee*, this year I'm doing kite flying with the *kinder*."

The trio made their way out from under the shade of the large oak tree and wandered over to the tables where Sadie's family was gathering. It was nice to see everyone. With her siblings getting married off and having *kinder*, her family was expanding. Her *bruder* William stood among the men chatting. He waved while Sadie joined the women. This was how it always was at these events, with everyone breaking off into groups.

Sadie joined Lizzie, Rachel and Sara under a shade tree. The four of them chatted for a bit about the weather and the school. Lizzie told them how good the store was doing and that her paintings were selling faster than she could paint them.

"The one of the fields where Paul and I had our first outing together is the most popular. We are looking into getting prints made. The *Englischers* like to have originals. But I have to charge so much for them. I'd really like to be able to price them so they are affordable for everyone who would like to buy my art."

"Lizzie, that is wonderful!" Rachel gave her a hug. "It's *gut* to hear of your success. My Jacob is so busy with the shed building that he's up at the crack of dawn and works by the light of the kerosene lamps at night.

He's thinking of asking Levi to stay on full-time as a partner."

Sadie's heartbeat kicked up a notch. The thought of Levi being a permanent part of the community meant that he liked being here. And maybe he wasn't going to be running off anytime soon.

"Levi has mentioned that the shop is busy," she said.

All heads swung in Sadie's direction.

She waved them off. "Stop looking at me like that. He told me because I asked for windows in the replacement shed they are building at the school," she explained, fighting back another blush.

What on earth has gotten into me today?

"He said he'd have to wait and see what Jacob had lying around. That's all." She tried to talk her way out of the conversation.

"Oh my." Sara looked at her intently. "You are smitten with Levi Byler."

"I am not," Sadie denied, even though she knew her sister's words had some merit. But there was no way she would admit the truth in front of them.

Out of the corner of her eye she caught a glimpse of Isaiah joining the group of men where her *vader* and *bruders* stood talking.

She glanced back to her sister and saw Sara's gaze following the man and knew then and there that Isaiah Troyer had the wrong Fischer *dochder* in his sights.

Sadie knew that, in time, everything would work out for all of them. They just had to be patient. Not one of her finer virtues. She had no intention of marrying Isaiah, and there was no reason why Sara shouldn't be with the one who would make him happy. Sadie only had to convince their *vader* of this. She had faith that everything would work out as it should. It had to.

The bell rang, and they followed the crowd over to the picnic tables.

Their family had managed to crowd in one place at the table. Sadie elbowed her way in between Sara and her sister-in-law Kara.

"It seems that the entire community has come out for this," Kara commented.

"Ja."

Across from them sat Rachel, Jacob and Levi, with Lizzie and Paul lining the bench next to Paul's family. Levi chatted with Paul. Sadie heard him ask a question about furniture making. And then her attention was pulled away as Sara told her it was their turn to go to the food line.

Sadie tried not to pile her plate high, but there were so many delectable choices. She was so busy walking through the line that she didn't realize Levi stood across from her until she recognized the sound of his voice speaking to one of the school board members.

Glancing up from her plate, she watched him, thinking what a good fit he'd be for their community.

"If you don't stop your gawking, people are going to start talking about you."

Sadie jumped and turned to Lizzie, who had come up behind her. Out of the side of her mouth, she whispered, "I wasn't gawking."

Lizzie leaned in close, talking low so only Sadie could hear. "*Ja*, I think you were. He's not too old, heaven forbid, not too young, and as far as I can tell, he doesn't appear to be in a relationship. He could be your perfect…"

Sadie nudged Lizzie with her elbow, cutting her off. "Stop. This isn't the time or the place for this discussion. There are too many *blabbermauls*."

Lizzie cocked her head to one side, the corner of her mouth lifting in a knowing way. And then she moved ahead of Sadie in the line. Feeling an unexpected flutter of nerves in her stomach and her appetite diminish,

Sadie left her spot in the line and went back to the picnic table. Some of her students came up to her along the way, telling her of their summer.

Little Mary Stolfus jumped up and down in front of Sadie, nearly knocking her plate out of her hand in her excitement to tell how she had gone fishing with her *bruders* for the first time.

"Mary, you could write a report on that for the class. I'm sure everyone would love to hear about your experience."

"Homework already!"

Sadie grinned down at the stricken look on the child's face. "Only if you wish to share. I'll tell you what. You can think about what you want to write and then when I give out the assignment, you'll be halfway done. How does that sound?"

"Like a *gut* idea." Mary clapped her hands together. "I've been practicing my letters with my *mamm*."

"You have?" Sadie's heart swelled. It was so wonderful to hear when her students took their learning seriously.

"Yup." Mary's blond head bobbed up and down.

"I'm very proud of you, Mary. I'll be flying kites after our meal. Come find me out in the lower field."

"I will, Miss Sadie!" With that, Mary ran off to join her friends.

Settling back in with her family, Sadie picked at her food.

Lizzie's words had left her with an odd feeling. She never wanted anyone, most of all Levi, to ever think that she was chasing after him, or any other man for that matter. Sadie wasn't like that. But she did know what she wanted, and she knew in her heart she would never settle for anything less. Shouldn't it be everyone's goal to find true happiness?

The minute the thought entered her head, she found herself face-to-face with Levi.

Chapter Eleven

Levi didn't think he'd ever tasted anything quite as delicious as Sadie's snickerdoodle cookies. He took a second bite, savoring the sweet, vanilla taste, and the sprinkle of sugar and cinnamon over the entire cookie was almost too much to bear.

"I see you're enjoying my cookies," Sadie observed from her side of the table.

"I am. And you know what I think?"

"I don't."

"I think there's a reason these won the blue ribbon."

"They've won the award on more than one occasion. I don't enter them in the bake-off anymore. It was time to give someone else a turn at the ribbon."

"Can you give me the recipe for my *mudder*?"

"I'll write it out for you and you can send it to her in your next letter."

"I'm sure she'll like that."

He noticed her plate sitting half-eaten off to one side and wondered if she was feeling okay.

Seeing his look, she commented, "My eyes were bigger than my stomach. There was so much good food on the tables that I wanted to try it all."

"The women in Miller's Crossing sure know how to cook. My stomach is full." He gave his belly a pat.

Sadie gave him one of her pretty smiles, saying, "But there's always room for dessert."

"Always," he agreed. He gave her a half smile.

"I've heard that Jacob is serious about wanting you to stay on."

The bluntness of her statement caught him off guard and wiped the smile off his face. One thing Levi knew for sure was that news in small communities traveled fast, and Miller's Crossing was no exception. Sadie had been after him for days to talk more about his life and what brought him here. He wasn't ready to discuss those parts of his life. Even though the pain of his breakup was easing,

Levi didn't want to be caught up in another relationship that would leave him broken. He still wasn't able to trust enough to be sure about Sadie.

He still hadn't been able to figure out if Sadie was looking to settle down or simply looking to settle.

People were beginning to clear away their plates. Some wandered off to the creek, others gathered under the shade tree and some were getting ready to play a game of softball.

"Levi." She spoke his name so softly he almost didn't hear her.

"Ja."

"Will you be staying on?"

They were interrupted by a small girl whose exuberance brought a smile to his face.

"Miss Sadie, we're ready to fly the kites! Are you coming?"

Her gaze lingered on him. Levi wanted to tell her what she needed to hear. But he couldn't. He didn't trust himself to open his heart. Still, he found himself wishing the outcome could be different. Maybe they were meant to be only friends.

While he pondered that thought, Sadie accepted the outstretched hand of the girl.

Standing up, she gave him a look that told him she wasn't finished with this conversation.

"Levi! Do you want to play in the softball game?" William called out to him from the field. "We need an outfielder."

"Go," Sadie said. "Have fun with the men."

"All right. You have fun with your kite flying."

"Come on, Miss Sadie!" the little girl clamored, tugging Sadie away from him.

He walked with them partway to the field, then broke off and headed to the ball field. He watched her disappear over the rise, wondering what would have happened if he'd met her sooner.

"Miss Sadie! Look how high my kite is!" Mary exclaimed, jumping up and down next to her.

Raising her hand to shield her eyes from the sun, Sadie looked heavenward, watching the kite dip and flutter in the wind. The tail with the pink-and-orange strips trailed out behind it, spinning in the breeze.

"I'm not having much luck with mine," said another girl. Beth Miller frowned at the tangled mess at her feet.

"Come, let me see if we can get yours

going." Sadie walked through the blades of grass. Picking up Beth's kite and handing it to her, she instructed, "You need to hold it here at the crosspieces."

She took hold of Beth's little fingers, placing them where the cross pieces met and once she was certain the girl had a good hold on the kite, she added, "Now you run into the wind until the breeze captures your kite."

Beth looked up at her with wide, brown, doubt-filled eyes.

"Let's give it a try, shall we?"

Beth nodded and then, doing as she was told, ran like the wind. Her little legs pumped hard on the soft earth, and to her delight the paper kite got off the ground, sailing up into the blue sky. The other *kinder* who'd been watching and playing with their own kites let out a cheer.

Beth turned to Sadie, shouting, "I did it! I did it!"

And then without warning the kite lost its lift and fell out of the sky, landing halfway up an oak tree.

Sadie ran over to where Beth stood under the tree, crying.

"Oh. There, there, *liebling*." Sadie patted

her on the back. "Wipe away those tears. I'll get your kite for you."

Without a thought, she hoisted herself up onto a low branch where the tail of the kite was just out of her reach. The fabric bows swayed in front of her, flirting with her. Sadie stretched her body tall and extended her arm as far as she could. The kite tail danced against her fingertips. She just started to grasp the string when her foot slipped on the branch.

"Get down from that tree!"

The familiar voice startled her, and she gave a shout as she tumbled backward out of the tree.

Her breath whooshed out of her as she fell hard against Levi. She spun around to face him. What on earth was he doing down here? She'd thought he was playing ball.

Oh my... Her heart skipped a beat as she looked up into his blue-green eyes. He looked frightened for a moment, and then she saw something else as he stared down at her. His gaze softened, taking in her face. His eyes lingered on hers and then his gaze dropped to her mouth. Sadie's breath caught.

Then he blinked and quick as a breeze the look was gone.

In the next instant she jumped out of his arms. She put her hand against the tree trunk to steady herself. Her heartbeat fluttered in her chest, and that fluttering had nothing to do with fear.

"Sadie! What were you doing up there?" he demanded.

"I was helping Beth get her kite out of the tree."

"You should have had one of the boys go up."

"I'll have you know, Levi, that I'm perfectly capable of climbing a tree."

"I don't doubt that, but when you have help nearby, you should ask."

She closed her eyes to keep her frustration from showing. How could he make her want to be near him one minute and then in the next make her so mad? Sadie swallowed, realizing she wasn't really mad at him, just unsettled by these feelings that popped up inside her whenever they were close to each other.

It would do no good to be flustered in front of the *kinder.* And in front of their parents who had made their way down the hill to see what all the commotion was about. Sadie's heart raced as she glanced at the faces of her neighbors, many of whom had known her for her entire life. And many of whom would like nothing more than to have something to gossip about during the next quilting bee.

It wouldn't do to have the schoolteacher be the fodder for their chatter. Sadie knew she should put her reputation first. But how did she do that while keeping her growing feelings toward Levi at bay?

Pushing away from the tree, she squared her shoulders. "You are absolutely correct." Putting on her sweetest smile, she asked, "Would you mind going up the tree and getting Beth's kite for her? Please."

"I'd be happy to."

He was up and back in less than three minutes, handing the kite to a very happy Beth, who took it from him.

"What do you say to Mr. Byler, Beth?"

"*Danke* for getting my kite out of the tree."

"Du bischt willkomm." Levi smiled at the little girl.

The smile brought out the fine lines at the corners of his eyes and a dimple on the left side of his mouth. The look suited him. And Sadie wondered, as she had since the first day she'd met him, why those smiles were so rare.

He brushed the dust off of his dark pants and adjusted his straw hat.

"*Danke*, Levi, for coming along when you did," Sadie finally offered.

The smile disappeared.

Feeling the need to state her case once more, she said, "I didn't mean to scare anyone."

"I know you didn't." His tone softened. "Let's get back to the picnic."

She didn't understand his behavior toward her. One minute he was nice as pie and the next he was acting like he didn't want to be around her and then he was back to being nice again. There was something going on between them, and she felt Levi was battling with these same feelings. She didn't know how to reach out to him, how to deal with this new tension developing between them.

But Sadie was a firm believer in the Lord working in mysterious ways. Levi had been sent here for a reason.

She needed to find out why he was so driven to keep his distance from her. She had to know if there was something between them other than their shared desire to complete the repairs on the school property in time for the upcoming semester. Determination drove Sadie in her work, and her personal life was no different. One way or another, she would get to the bottom of this.

Levi walked ahead of her, leaving Sadie to accompany the *kinder* back up to the picnic tables. Lizzie came up to her, linking her arm through hers, and gave Sadie a reassuring pat on the hand.

"It seems Levi's rescue is drawing a bit of attention."

Sadie looked at her friend. "I saw the women watching us."

"Not just them, Sadie."

She followed Lizzie's pointed gaze, seeing where her concern came from. Sadie's *mamm* and *vader* stood on the knoll watching her walk up the hill. This would only make her *vader*'s case stronger for a match between her and Isaiah. Sadie had to find a way to head this off, and the sooner, the better.

Her parents met her at the top of the hill.

Her *mamm* rushed over to her. "Are you all right?"

"I'm fine. Levi was right there to break my fall. And even if he wasn't, I would have been perfectly capable of not getting hurt."

"You don't know that, Sadie," her *mamm* scolded. "You are always so impetuous."

"*Dochder*, it's time we packed up to head home."

She nodded at her *vader* and helped her *mamm* pick up their remaining leftovers. This day had left her a bundle of nerves. To hide the feeling, she busied her hands packing up the picnic basket and carrying it over to their buggy. Levi was helping Rachel and Jacob put their basket and softball equipment in the back of their buggy.

Spotting her, he waved.

Sadie waved back.

Off to her left stood her *vader*. She felt his gaze on them.

He came up behind her. "Come, let's get our things loaded up. We have evening chores to tend to." His voice sounded gruff.

A sinking feeling hit Sadie. Her time to be a part of deciding her future was running short.

Chapter Twelve

A week later Levi found himself face-to-face with Sadie's *vader.* The man had been waiting for him at the school.

"Levi, I'd like a word with you."

Drawing in a breath, Levi jumped down from the wagon seat. Pushing his hat back off his forehead, he walked over to Saul Fischer. The man straightened his shoulders. Levi stood a good head taller than him.

"What can I do for you, Saul?"

"I'm not going to beat around the bush. I'm here to talk to you about my *dochder* Sadie."

"I see," Levi said, knowing full well where this conversation would be heading.

"I'm not sure what she's told you about her future. But my Sadie wants things she can't have. Right now, her job is to teach the *kinder* of our community. And she's of the marrying age."

Narrowing his eyes, Levi looked at Sadie's *vader*, trying to figure out where he was going with his thoughts. Levi didn't want to make a decision he might later regret.

"When you are married with *kinder* of your own, you will understand that a *vader* knows what's right for his *dochders* and *sohns*. I've chosen someone for Sadie. He's a *gut*, solid man with a home that's ready for a wife."

Levi folded his arms across his chest, thinking he must look as though he had none of those traits. He thought he was a *gut* person, but he didn't really know what his future held. He supposed to Saul Fischer, he could look like something of a drifter. A man that wouldn't be a *gut* fit for his *dochder*.

He knew arranged marriages were not uncommon in their culture. But he doubted the Sadie he knew would ever settle for something like that. He couldn't imagine her living with a man she didn't love for the rest of her life.

Levi thought about him and Anne. He'd been so in love with her, and yet he'd come to find out she'd not returned those feelings...leastwise not for him. Now that time had passed, he knew they never would have been happy together. He wanted Sadie to be happy. Still, at this time he didn't think he'd be the right match for her.

But he'd seen Isaiah Troyer. He didn't think the man was a fit for Sadie either. He couldn't imagine her spending the rest of her life with him, bearing his children.

And those thoughts would do him no *gut*. "I understand what you are saying, Saul."

"Do you? I know how Sadie can turn things to her liking. But in this matter, I need her to abide by my wishes. I'm asking you to tread carefully where she is concerned. You would do well to remember her standing as the teacher in our community. She has a reputation to uphold. You two have been working here these past weeks, many times alone. If nothing else, I want you to steer clear of her."

With that, the man turned and boarded his wagon, leaving Levi to his work and his thoughts.

He should have told Saul that he needn't worry. Levi had no plans to rush into any kind of a relationship. He and Sadie were friends, nothing more. At least that was what he kept telling himself.

He'd barely had time to unpack his work

tools when another wagon came into the schoolyard. This one carrying Sadie's *bruders* William and John. William jumped down from the wagon and came over to him.

"Levi! *Gut* to see you again."

"You, too."

"John and I were going fishing today on Lake Erie. We were wondering if you'd want to join us."

He declined the invitation and sent them on their way. There was no time to take a day off, not if he hoped to get everything completed on schedule. And he suspected that William and John were trying to learn more about him.

He expected nothing less of them. He'd have done the same for his sisters when they were getting ready to be married off. The difference here was Levi had no intention of asking for Sadie's hand in marriage.

Picking up the hammer, he pounded the nail into the piece of siding he'd been putting up on the back of the shed. The wood was stubborn and he had to strike the nail three times before the head settled snuggly against the hearty oak slab siding. He slid the next piece of wood into place, continuing to pound the nails. Maybe if he worked hard enough and long enough, he could ease the thoughts of Sadie Fischer out of his mind.

But that was becoming harder to do. As each day passed, he wondered how the classroom was coming along. Levi knew better than to approach Sadie if she was working alone. Jacob had warned him off, and Levi suspected the elders were concerned that he and Sadie were spending too much time alone, even if it were for the *gut* of the *kinder*. And now with the visits from her *vader* and her *bruders*, he took these warnings to heart. Sadie was a respected member of her community and she didn't need any trouble coming from him.

Still, he found himself missing the sound of her voice and the way she laughed at the simple things. He envied the way she could be so carefree even when he'd seen the hard days she'd had. Sadie was well liked by her students and their families. These were all *gut* qualities. He smiled, thinking about how patient she'd been with the little girl at the picnic. Sadie could easily have flown that kite herself and then handed the string to the girl. Instead she'd taught the girl how to fly the kite.

The phrase *give a man a fish and you feed*

him for a day; teach a man to fish and you feed him for a lifetime came to mind.

Nothing seemed to get Sadie down. She clearly loved her job and all of the *kinder* she taught. They adored her. That had been clear when they'd all come around her during the picnic.

She was a kind, decent person. Not what he expected to find when he'd come here. Sadie was nothing like his former fiancée. Though Anne had seemed committed to their relationship, it turned out she'd had other plans all along. He knew Sadie's life was firmly grounded here in Miller's Crossing. But that didn't mean he wasn't going to keep exercising caution where she was concerned.

There would be no more impulsive decisions when it came to finding love. Perhaps he needed to be forceful with his intentions where Sadie was concerned. If he told her there could be nothing between them other than friendship, maybe that would take some of this pressure off of them. He didn't want to be the cause of her losing her job. In his mind, it was too soon to have feelings for her, even though, no matter how hard he tried to deny it, his heart had begun to open up to her.

The one sure thing in his life was his faith

in the Lord. Time and time again the Lord had provided for him in his moments of need. Pausing, he turned his attention to the Lord, asking for guidance and giving thanks for what he already had.

As he carried on with his duties, Levi worked in silence, stuck within his own thoughts, until he heard Sadie calling out to him.

"Levi? I know you're out here. I've heard your hammering all morning."

"I'm around back," he called out.

Putting his hammer into his leather tool belt, he walked around to meet Sadie.

All of his thoughts about using caution flew out of his mind the minute he saw her. She looked even prettier today than the last time he'd seen her. Her face had a healthy glow from being outside in the summer sunshine. She wore one of her famous smiles. She held a white envelope.

Narrowing his eyes, he focused on that, rather than on how lovely her blue eyes appeared today. "What do you have there?"

"My blue-ribbon snickerdoodle recipe, just like I promised."

"*Danke.* I know my *mamm* will enjoy making them. I'll send it along with my next letter."

He stood there, gazing into her eyes. His thoughts swirled around in his mind once again. Sadie deserved better than what he could offer. His heart had been broken and was barely mended. Maybe the breakup had been because of something he'd done…something he may be doomed to repeat. The last thing he wanted was to hurt Sadie. They'd already breached propriety by working without others around them. Levi recognized the fact that Sadie's job was important to her. Neither one of them should be putting her future in jeopardy.

Perhaps if she could see his flaws when it came to love, she would go back to focusing on her teaching.

"Levi?"

"Ja?"

"Are you going to take the envelope?"

"Sure, sure." In two strides, he closed the gap between them. Careful to keep his distance at arm's length, he accepted the recipe.

"This is coming along," Sadie observed as she took her time meandering to the other side of the building. Stopping in front of the shed, she turned to him. "*Danke* for the windows."

"Jacob found some extras."

"Admit it, Levi, this project is much better with the windows. Just think of all the plants my *kinder* and I can start out here. The light is perfect!"

"You were right in your thinking."

"I'm glad we can agree on that." She let out a laugh, clapping her hands together in triumph. "I can picture all those seedlings tilting toward the sunlight. This year I'm planning on doing more flowers. We need to replace the plants that were damaged in the storm anyway. We can start with the pansies and Johnny-jump-ups. Then we can move on to the marigolds and mums. I can just see their yellow and orange blooms lining the bushes around the front of the building."

"You're planning way ahead of the next spring season," he commented, realizing he'd grown used to hearing her talk in long segments.

"It doesn't hurt to plan or to use your imagination and dream about what something could look like."

They grew quiet. Off in the distance, a tractor engine started up. A few cars drove by the schoolyard. Sadie stilled. She looked up at him, her gaze taking in every inch of his face. By now he recognized that look. Sadie wanted more from him.

Levi swallowed. He needed to tell her there could be nothing more between them. "You got something on your mind, Sadie?"

Rolling her shoulders back, Sadie took her time forming her words. She'd been thinking about this moment ever since the picnic. Now the time had arrived, and she found herself feeling the unthinkable: tongue-tied.

Levi looked at her with one dark eyebrow cocked, his mouth in a firm line. She wondered if he thought she might be about to scold him for something.

Nee, this wasn't the case. She needed to talk to him about their relationship. Sadie knew she wasn't alone in sensing the undercurrent running between them. Her friends and her family had mentioned their observations to her. If others saw it, then there had to be more to it than just her wishful thinking.

"Levi, I..." She hesitated. This was going to be harder than she'd thought. Then she reminded herself how long she'd been fighting her *vader* over the Isaiah issue. If she wanted to have any hope of finding happiness in her future, then she needed to be brave.

"Levi, why are you here?"

A surprised look crossed his face. Then he asked, "Here? As in here at the school?"

"*Nee*, Levi. I think you know what I meant by my question."

She saw realization dawn on him.

"Ah. Here as in Miller's Crossing."

"*Ja.*"

He toyed with the handle on the hammer in his tool belt. Sadie watched as he grew still again, his hands dropping to his sides. His eyes took on a deeper shade of green as he pondered her request. She wanted to grab hold of him and shake the words out. Why was he so stubborn when it came to talking about his past? What was he afraid of? Sadie wasn't some monster who wanted to hurt him. She did, however, long to know if he had been feeling the same way she had.

"I don't have time for whatever this is, Sadie. There's a lot of work yet to be done if my job is to be completed on time."

She stood even taller. "Levi, I'll ask you again. Why are you here? Surely you have a family who misses you and would like you to return to their community."

"Sadie."

There was a plea in his voice. She heard

it, and her heart broke for whatever pain he was suffering. Whether or not he wanted to believe it, he had become a part of Miller's Crossing. Levi wasn't just some worker passing through. The *kinder* liked him. Her *bruders* had even begun to change their idea about the man. Otherwise they never would have invited him to go along on their fishing trip.

"Every time I think we're about to grow closer, you shut me off. Why is that, Levi?"

"Sadie!"

He looked shocked at her forwardness, but she didn't have time to waste wondering if whatever was happening between them was simply a figment of her imagination. Desperation was creeping in.

"Please, Levi. Tell me."

"Sadie…" He extended a hand to her. "Don't. Move."

"Why?"

Levi seemed to be focused on something behind her. Suddenly afraid, Sadie started to turn her head.

"Levi, what is going on?"

He brought his finger to his lips. Very carefully, he mouthed, "Skunk."

Sadie's mouth formed an O. She heard the animal rustling around behind her. Levi's hand grabbed her forearm as they both held their breath. Sadie tried not to notice how warm his fingertips felt or the way his steady pulse thrummed beside her.

She didn't know how much time passed. Seconds turned into minutes.

And then he released her.

He gave his head a shake and grinned down at her. "That was a close call."

Her hand flew up to cover her heart. "You can say that again! *Danke* for saving me. Oh, my goodness, I can't even think about how bad that would have been if the skunk had sprayed us."

Blinking up at him, she went on, "Last year one of our dogs got into it with a skunk in the back field. We went through a case of canned tomato juice trying to get that smell off him. *Gut* thing the grocery store had them on sale or else we would have had to empty out the pantry!"

Levi turned away from her. "Perhaps we should get back to work."

"Levi, can't we at least finish our conversation?" Sadie sucked in her lower lip, waiting on his answer, holding out hope.

"I'm not sure that's a *gut* idea."

"Why?"

"Because."

She put her hands on her hips and glared up at him. "As I tell my students, *because* is not an answer.

"All right. How about because I can't tell you what you want to hear? The last thing I want to do is hurt you, Sadie. You've no idea how hard a relationship can be."

Sadie let his words sink in. "I know you would never hurt me." And then it dawned on her. "But you… You've been hurt by someone."

It was not a question. The soul-crushing look on his face told part of his story.

He shook his head as if to clear away the pain. "Please, don't push me on this."

She bit down on her lip, her heart breaking for him. She couldn't imagine anyone hurting a man so kind and giving. "I'm not pushing you."

"*Ja*, you are." His voice rose in anger. "It's like you're on some sort of self-imposed timeline." He paused, clenching his teeth together. Then his look softened. "I know your *vader* has someone in mind for you. Maybe you should consider his choice. Sadie, I'm not sure I'm the man who can be your 'not too old or not too young.'"

Her mouth fell open. He'd overheard the conversation she and Lizzie had had weeks ago, and those words had stayed with him. Sadie was ashamed at their silliness. She and Lizzie had been joking. But deep down, Sadie knew the words carried some certainty. She didn't want to settle. She wanted her own happily-ever-after. Even if he thought differently right now, Sadie knew she could have that with the man who stood before her.

"The day is getting on," he said. "We'd best be getting back to work."

She knew when to let something go, but this time she just couldn't leave it be. While Levi had built up a wall around his emotions that might seem impenetrable, she knew better. Her faith and her instincts were stronger than ever. This wasn't over yet.

"I don't understand why you are being so stubborn."

"Because you could lose your job over this," he said, waving his hand back and forth between them.

"Why do you say that?"

"Because we both know you're under scrutiny right now. Your position has not been made permanent."

"You don't need to remind me of that, Levi."

"Sadie, there is so much about me that you don't know."

"Then tell me," she pleaded.

He shook his head, making her angry and sad at the same time. "This isn't the time for us to begin anything other than a friendship."

His words stung. "You can't mean that." Sadie felt her lower lip tremble.

"Your *vader* has someone picked out for you. Perhaps it would be best if you went with his choice."

"That's a terrible thing to say to me," Sadie said, trying not to cry in front of him.

"I only want what is best for you. First off, your job here is part of who you are. I can't be the reason that would be taken from you. Second, we've only known each other a short amount of time."

"You don't always need a lot of time to know when something feels right."

"Sadie, please don't make this any harder than it needs to be."

She put her hand over her heart, trying to hold back the pain. She wasn't ready to give up. She wouldn't give in this easily. Deep in her heart, she knew they were right together. Isaiah Troyer wasn't the Amish man for her. Levi was.

Sadie tried one more tactic before letting him leave. "Levi, promise me one thing."

He stopped walking and looked over one shoulder at her. "What?"

"Promise me you'll think about this. The Lord brought you here for a reason."

His eyes clouded with emotion. Sadie could almost see the tiny break in the shell he'd put around his heart.

"I'll consider your words." With a shrug, he added, "I can offer you nothing more."

Brushing a tear from her eye, she watched him go. "Hope," she whispered. "You've offered me hope."

Chapter Thirteen

He felt like the worst of the worst, and burying himself in his work did little to alleviate that feeling. Ever since the conversation with Sadie, Levi had been taking on every extra hour of work he could get from Jacob and then some. He figured by keeping his hands and his mind busy, he wouldn't have time to think about Sadie. But just the opposite had happened. By cutting himself off from the community, he'd only had time to think.

Time to think about him and this woman who'd come into his life like a tornado. Her enthusiasm for life couldn't be missed. He envied her patience with her students and the way she'd thrown herself into getting her classroom ready for the new school year. She could be so carefree even when he knew she'd had a hard day.

Sadie was a force to be reckoned with, and the problem was Levi didn't know what to do with his feelings for her. He'd taken the coward's way out when she'd been brave enough to broach the subject of their relationship. He'd been nothing but honest with her, even though he didn't think he'd ever be able to share with her what Anne had done to him. The pain she'd caused, the way she'd ruined his trust and taken away his faith in finding true love.

He walked down the drive to the shed company from Jacob's house. Levi wasn't certain where his life was headed. One thing he knew for sure, he didn't like being in limbo.

Grabbing the doorknob, he pulled the side door open. The scent of fresh-cut lumber wafted by him. Some workers were busy doing finishing work, while others were on the assembly line putting together the framing for the walls.

No doubt about it, Jacob's business was booming.

"Levi! Just the person I've been looking for." Jacob headed toward him, removing his safety glasses and hearing protection. He clapped Levi on the shoulder. "Come on into my office."

Levi followed him and took the seat Jacob offered.

"How's all of this going for you?" his friend asked.

"*Gut*. Except for a few paint touch-ups, I'm finished at the school." Levi didn't feel the relief he'd expected over completing the job. It meant he'd no longer have a reason to see Sadie every day. The thought sent a jolt of surprise through him.

"Listen, Levi. There's something I've been wanting to discuss with you."

"Okay."

"I know you came here for temporary work. But my orders are not slowing down. Right now, I have half a dozen landscape and nursery companies owned by *Englischers* looking to stock my sheds, in addition to Troyer's big nursery right here in Clymer. And I've got more asking about the sheds."

Pushing his hat back on his head, Levi said, "You've been blessed, my cousin."

"I have been. These people don't want stock assembly line–type products. They are clamoring for Amish made."

Levi sat up taller in the chair. "I'm not sure what you're asking here, Jacob."

Steepling his fingers, Jacob speared him with a look of determination. "I want to share my blessings with you."

"I don't know what that means, exactly."

"It means I want you to go into partnership with me."

Levi settled against the back of the chair in shock. Though he'd known Jacob and Rachel had been discussing this, he'd no idea that a full partnership was what his cousin had been thinking about. Levi had expected the possibility of more hours, taking on more responsibility within the shop or maybe even overseeing projects, but this… He'd not seen this offer coming.

A partnership.

This could be life changing. Of course, it would mean relocating here permanently. He knew one person who would be delighted with this bit of news. He so wished this opportunity had come along even a year ago. But then, he reminded himself, a year ago he wasn't even considering leaving his community to start fresh. Now with his life in limbo, he had no idea what he wanted. Could this be the answer to his prayers, or would taking Jacob up on his offer only bring more heartache?

"Hey, Levi. I can see from the look on your face that my offer hasn't brought you the happiness I'd hoped for."

"*Nee, nee.* It's not that. I've so much on my mind, Jacob. So much to consider. And you and Rachel have been so kind to me these past weeks."

"Well, we like having you here. And you've been a tremendous help for me. And my Rachel likes having me home a few nights a week in time for supper." Jacob leaned forward. "Is there something else I don't know about?"

Levi knew the gossip concerning him and Sadie was quietly making its way around Miller's Crossing. Things like the prospect of a new couple never stayed quiet for long in any close-knit town, particularly an Amish one. Right now, he told himself, there was nothing more between them than a growing friendship, though he knew Sadie wanted more. Levi didn't know if he had it in him to give her that. He'd tried to explain that to her when he'd seen her last.

Maybe he was nothing but a coward when it came to love.

"Levi?" Jacob's voice interrupted his musings. "What do you think?"

"I'm not sure."

"If this helps any, I'm aware of the undercurrent between you and Sadie. I know it's none of my business, but if that's holding you back—"

"Jacob, I came here because I needed time to put my life back in order." Levi gave his cousin the short version of what had transpired between him and Anne. "I thought I'd found the love of my life last year and she ended up leaving me. I'm not sure I can be this man Sadie is searching for."

He knew he'd hurt her feelings the other day. He felt terrible about it.

"For what it's worth," Jacob said at last, "I think the Lord knows what He's doing and He sent you here for a reason other than to help out a family member and a friend."

"Funny those are the words you chose. Sadie said the same thing… Well, the part about the Lord bringing me here for a reason."

"You should listen to her." Jacob smiled. "So, you'll think about my offer?"

"I will."

"Levi, I really want to make this work. If

you decide to leave, then I'll have to seek out someone else to buy into a partnership. I really want to keep this business in the family."

"I understand."

"One more piece of advice—you need to let go of your past. Otherwise you'll never find the happiness you deserve."

Levi knew the bigger part of this would be not only letting go of the past, but letting Sadie in. He wondered if he could find the courage do that.

Sadie stepped out the front door of the schoolhouse, taking in the glorious sight spread out before her. The fall semester had gotten underway a few days ago, and Sadie had been thankful for the distraction of preparing for this week. It kept her mind off of Levi. She hadn't seen him since the day he'd told her he couldn't be the one for her.

So now Sadie filled her time with teaching. Watching her students, both young and old, playing in the schoolyard filled her heart with gladness. The swings were full with the *kinder.* And the older ones ran around the bases playing a raucous game of kickball. She hated to end their freedom, but the lessons were calling. She yanked a braided string and rang the bell.

"Come on, everyone. The quicker you get inside, the quicker you can get to your work!"

Mary stepped out of the line, asking, "Miss Sadie, did you see how high I went on the swing?"

"I did, Mary. You've really improved."

"*Danke*, Miss Sadie."

She ushered the rest of the *kinder* inside. "I hope you all enjoyed your time outside. And now that we've settled in our seats, I want to go over the chore list with you." In addition, she had a special project for them to work on.

There were a few groans. She stayed behind her desk, waiting for them to quiet. "I've assigned the tasks based on what I think you can do best. You'll find your name on the sheet and then be responsible for that chore."

Mica's hand shot up. "What if we don't like the chore?"

"Then you'll do your best to complete it. Now, today I'd like us to start on our first class project of the school term. As you know, our building and shed sustained some damage over the summer from that storm. I'd like to break off into groups—the boys in one, the girls in the other. We are going to make thank-you cards for Mr. Byler and Mr. Herschberger. The girls will work on one for Mr. Byler and the boys will do the one for Mr. Herschberger. They did a great deal to make sure your classroom was ready for you. In addition, Mr. Byler built us a brand-new shed. When the cards are finished, you can each take a turn signing your name."

Sadie had already set up large pieces of paper on the project table located along the side wall. "Perhaps some of you older boys can help move the table away from the wall so there is space for you to gather around. "We'll have the girls work first since there won't be room for all of you at once. In the meantime, I'd like the boys to get out their chapter books and begin reading silently."

After she got the girls set up with paper, crayons and colored pencils, she walked around the room, helping the boys with their reading. She stopped by Josh's desk and worked with him to sound out a word, but when she got to Mica's desk, she noticed he hadn't even opened his book.

"Mica, why aren't you reading?"

He gave a shrug. "I have a headache."

Concerned, she inspected his face, then lay her hand lightly against his forehead, looking for any signs of a fever. "Would you like me to get you a cold compress to put on your forehead? That might help."

"Nee."

"All right. Stay here and rest at your desk. I'll keep an eye on you."

"*Danke*, Miss Sadie."

Moving down the line, she stopped a few more times to work with the other students. Noticing a half hour had passed, she switched the groups out. The girls were quick to open their books.

"Mary Ellen, could you please take little Mary and Beth over to the reading corner and read out loud to them?"

"Yes, Miss Sadie."

Mary Ellen was one of her oldest students and soon she would be aging out of the classroom. Next year, she'd finish up eighth grade. Sadie intended to have her assist her with the other *kinder* this year. The girl loved to learn and had an abundance of patience. Sadie hoped she might go into teaching.

She heard chatter coming from the craft table and went over to check on the progress the boys were making with their card. Oddly enough, Mica was bent over the table with a crayon in his hand coloring in some lettering.

He elbowed Josh, who leaned in, cupped his hand and whispered into Mica's ear.

She found Mica's behavior odd, considering he'd just told her he couldn't read because he had a headache. She'd believed him and allowed him to skip his reading time. She might come off as a kind and easygoing teacher, but Sadie didn't like being lied to.

She needed to nip this in the bud.

"Mary Ellen, I need you to stop reading to the girls and keep an eye on the class."

Stepping behind Mica, she gave him a pat on the shoulder. "Mica, I'd like to have a word with you, outside."

She knew from the look on his face that he understood he was in trouble. A hush fell over the room as she led him out the back door, where her steps faltered as she came face-to-face with Levi.

"Levi! What are you doing here?"

"I'm finishing up with the painting on the shed. How are you doing, Sadie?"

"I'm fine. And yourself?"

She wanted to shake some sense into him. Here they were speaking to each other like they were polite strangers, when they both knew better. Mica squirmed. She'd nearly forgotten he was standing beside her.

"Mica, sit on the step, please, while I speak to Mr. Byler."

Doing as he was told, the boy sat on the bottom step awaiting his fate.

"I'm doing okay."

Longing to ask if he missed her as much as she'd been missing him, Sadie forced herself to watch Mica as he brought his knees up to his chest. Wrapping his arms around his legs, he rested his chin on his bony little kneecaps. Sadie didn't like to think that he might be afraid of his punishment. She had no intention of being overly strict. That wasn't her way.

She glanced over his head at the shed. It looked mighty nice with the spotless windows flanking either side of the door, and the whitewashed siding. Levi had done a fine job.

"The shed looks wonderful, Levi."

"*Danke.* I have one last thing to do and then I'm done."

She wondered if he felt the same pain she felt. A knot had formed in the pit of her stomach. She didn't know what to do with the sensations rippling through her. How could she, upon seeing him here, feel joy and sadness at the same time? Even after their last conversation, even after the days of feeling hurt and empty inside, why did her heartbeat still kick up at the sight of him? Sadie knew then and there whatever was between them hadn't ended as Levi had wanted.

The sound of the *kinder*'s voices coming from behind her jolted her back to reality.

"I'd like to drop by Jacob and Rachel's on my way home," she said to Levi. "Could you let them know to expect me?"

"Ja."

"Miss Sadie, can I go back inside?"

"*Nee*, Mica. We need to talk." She looked back up to find Levi watching her, the expression on his face carefully guarded. Sadie fought hard to tamp down her frustration with the man. This situation infuriated her and she didn't know how to fix it.

"I'll leave you to your day," Levi said.

He walked off, leaving her to watch his retreating back. The breeze ruffled the dark locks of hair skimming the top of his blue work shirt. Sadie took in his tall, lanky form, remembering the first day they'd met and what a mess she'd been.

She wanted to cry.

"Miss Sadie? Are you okay?" Mica asked.

She took in a deep breath, bolstering her courage. Looking down at the boy, she gave him a shaky smile. "I'm fine, *danke*." Gathering her skirt, she sat next to him. "Mica, I know you understand that lying, even a tiny fib, is wrong."

He nodded.

"I'm going to let you off easy this time around by sending your reading home with you tonight. You can read the pages and we'll discuss them tomorrow. I'll send a note to your parents so they'll know. I won't mention why."

He swiped a hand across his eyes. It broke her heart to see any of her students in pain.

"Mica, do as I've asked and all will be well."

"Okay, Miss Sadie. I'll try."

She patted him on his thin shoulder as they stood. Holding the door open, Sadie let Mica go inside ahead of her. She had one foot on the threshold when she thought she'd heard her name.

Turning, she saw Levi about to swing his hammer against a piece of wood. She waited, hoping he'd stop and look at her. But he didn't.

Squaring her shoulders, she followed Mica inside, closing the door behind them. She wanted to do nothing more than sit at her desk and lament over Levi. But there wasn't time to do that. She had a class to tend to.

The rest of the day flew by with math lessons and their first English assignment, which was to write about what they did over summer break. While they worked on that, she wrote the note to Mica's parents. She let Mary Ellen lead the class in the closing scripture, and then made sure each of them had signed their name to the thank-you cards.

Once the *kinder* were gone, Sadie neatened up her desk, grabbed the cards and, locking the door behind her, went to where she'd left her bicycle. She put the cards in the basket on the handrails and headed for Jacob and Rachel's.

The trip took about half an hour, and Sadie had been preparing herself for the final hill the entire time. Back in her younger days, she'd been able to ride up the steep incline with little effort. But now it loomed like an unscalable mountain in front of her.

Resting her feet on either side of the bike, she pondered the situation. She could easily get off and walk the bike up the hill, or she could take on the challenge to ride. While she stood there debating, she heard the creaking of a wagon coming up behind her. She turned to see if it might be someone she knew.

"Hey, do you need a lift?"

The bobbing of her head said one thing while her mouth said, "Nope. I'm *gut*."

Cocking his head to one side, Levi asked, "Are you sure? Seems like you're having trouble deciding."

She scuffed the toe of her foot along the side of the road, trying to make up her mind. If she remained stubborn and pushed the bike up the hill, it would be at least another twenty minutes before she arrived at Rachel and Jacob's place. Then the time for a visit would be shortened because she still had to pedal back to her house, which would get her home just in time for supper. But if she took Levi up on his offer, she'd have more time to visit with Rachel.

On the other hand, she didn't understand why he wanted to be with her. He'd made his feelings on their relationship clear. She didn't need to spend any more time with this man. A man who didn't want her to be a part of his life.

"Come on, Sadie, let me give you a ride."

Chapter Fourteen

He could almost see her mind working at coming up with a reason not to go with him. But finally, she got off the bike and took some papers out of the basket. She let him take hold of the handlebars. While she got herself seated in the wagon, he loaded the bike in the back.

Grabbing hold of the side rail to hoist himself up, Levi observed, "Maybe your *vader* should let you get one of those motorized scooters." Settling next to her, he added, "The youngies go whizzing by me all the time."

"*Nee.* He thinks they are too dangerous. And they sort of frighten me. Today I'm heading to see Rachel and to drop off a surprise for you and Jacob," she explained, keeping her eyes straight ahead on the road.

"What sort of surprise?"

"If I told you, it wouldn't be a surprise." She held her hands neatly over the papers in her lap.

Apparently, she would not be elaborating, so he asked, "Did Mica get into trouble?"

"I wouldn't call it trouble. We had a misunderstanding."

"I see. He's a *gut* boy."

"He is."

Levi understood Sadie's stiff attitude toward him and yet it still stung. He knew he'd been the one to put a halt to their feelings. It had been the right thing to do for both of them. She'd be free to find someone who could love her with his whole heart, and Levi…

Well, he didn't know what any of this meant for him. He'd done a lot of thinking about what Jacob had said.

Putting aside the hurt and pain of betrayal had taken a toll on his soul. And now he had this offer of a partnership from his cousin. An opportunity that, if he accepted, would mean he'd be living near Sadie. He'd see her at church services and picnics. He didn't imagine she'd be single much longer. Levi might have to reconcile himself to seeing her with someone else. Then again, he'd told her to move on, to accept the man her *vader* had chosen.

Knowing Sadie, though, he doubted she had any plans to settle on a choice that wasn't of her own making. His heart ached. Somehow this ache didn't feel the same as what he'd felt when Anne had left him. *Nee*, this pain held something different. A longing that didn't seem to go away. Sadie was literally within arm's reach. He knew all he had to do was turn and tell her his words had been a mistake.

He wouldn't do that. Sadie deserved someone who could love her with their heart intact. Levi didn't trust himself with his feelings. The hurt and pain of Anne's betrayal still lingered, and he couldn't seem to let go.

"Levi?" Her warm, sweet voice broke through his musings. *"Bischt allrecht?"*

"Ja," he answered, even though he felt far from all right. Clearing his throat, he noted, "We're here. Shall I drop you at the house?"

"I'd like that, *danke*. But I do have that surprise for you. So, come inside with me."

She waited for him on the porch as he tied the horse to the hitching post. The afternoon sunlight spilled across the house, bathing her in a warm glow making his heart ache all over again. Sadie had to be the prettiest woman he'd ever seen.

Rachel burst onto the porch. "Sadie! I'm so happy to see you. I just made some iced *kaffi*. Jacob and Levi have been partaking at the end of these hot days. Would you like a glass?"

"Just water, please, Rachel."

"I'll bring out some of my sugar *kichlins*, too. I'm afraid they do not compare to your snickerdoodles," Rachel admitted with a laugh.

She headed back into the house, and Levi heard her call out to Jacob, telling him they were here. A shadow appeared behind the screen. Jacob swung the door open and came out to join them.

"*Gute nammidaag*, Sadie. Levi."

"*Gute nammidaag* to you, Jacob," Sadie replied, sitting in one of the rockers on the porch. "I've brought you and Levi a surprise from the *kinder*."

"*Ach*. We don't need a surprise." Jacob raised his hands in front of his chest.

"This is one you will cherish, I promise."

After pulling two folded sheets of paper out of an envelope, she handed one to Jacob.

Levi stepped around him to collect the remaining one Sadie held out to him. His fingertips skimmed hers. For the briefest of moments, her soft skin brushed against his roughened hands. She pulled away, casting her eyes downward. His stomach clenched. What had he done?

"Rachel. Come see this card the *kinder* made." Jacob's face lit up with joy. "Show me yours, Levi."

Levi held the paper between his fingers. The *kinder* had indeed done a fine job with their artwork. The front of his card had a rather rustic drawing of the shed. He smiled when he saw the stick figures alongside. Each one had an arrow pointing at it. One had the name *Mica* written over it and the other *Josh*. Levi shook his head. He'd never forget working with those boys. Opening the card, he read each name. *Thank you* was written in block letters.

He'd never gotten a gift such as this. He looked up to find Sadie watching him. Her blue eyes taking in his face, she gave him a slight nod.

"I told you, you would like this surprise."

"You were right."

"Here's our refreshments!" Rachel came

out onto the porch carrying a tray of drinks and the plate of *kichlin*.

"Sadie, did Levi tell you his news?" she asked, as she handed out the drinks.

Accepting the ice water, Sadie answered, "*Nee.*"

"Jacob has officially asked him to become a partner in the business. This is such *gut* news for us. Of course, he has to say yes first."

Sadie's mouth opened and then closed. Setting her glass on the low table between the rockers, she rose, brushing past Levi.

"I'm afraid it's later than I thought. I'd best be getting home. *Danke* for the water, Rachel."

Setting his glass next to hers, Levi hurried down the porch steps after her. "Sadie, let me take you home."

She spun around so fast they bumped into each other.

She started to push him away. "I can get myself home. Don't worry about me. My house is downhill from here."

"Sadie, I know you're upset with Rachel's news."

Keeping her voice low so Rachel and Jacob

couldn't overhear, she barely got out, "Rachel's news? Is that how you think of this? Jacob offered you the partnership, Levi. You." She poked a finger against his chest.

He started to take hold of her hand. Feeling as if her skin had been scorched, she took a step back, out of his reach. It seemed that no matter what he did and said to her these days, it only ended in pain and hurt. Sadie didn't know how to get him to see that together they could make anything work. Why did he continue to hold back?

"I have to go." With that, she made her way to where he'd left her bike leaning up against the side of the wagon.

"Don't go off angry."

Slowing her pace, she turned to face him.

His hands were clenched at his sides. Sadie longed to take hold of them, to feel his strength, to offer him hope. But she stood there, waiting for him to say something, anything, realizing if he were to stay here in Miller's Crossing that their lives would become intertwined.

Her heartbeat settled into a calmer rhythm as her anger dissipated. If Levi took Jacob's offer, he would be here, near her. She dared to meet his gaze, wondering if any of this had occurred to him. Wondering if he even cared. His steadfastness told her he did.

"I can't be late for dinner again."

And she rode off, arriving home to find her *vader* waiting for her. He sat on the front porch in his favorite chair, sipping from a glass of lemonade. She noticed his hands and the calluses etched in them from the years working in the fields. A straw hat covered his graying hair. His mouth was pulled into a grim line. Stepping up onto the porch, Sadie avoided his gaze.

"*Dochder.* Come, *sittsit unnah.* It's time for us to talk."

She knew better than to disobey him, even though she knew full well what he wanted to talk about. She sat on the hard bench next to the door.

"I can't wait any longer for you to make up your mind. I want a union between you and Isaiah Troyer. It will be good to bring both households together."

Her stomach twisted at his words. "Please, *Daed.* I only need a little more time."

"I've given you time. Sadie, you are the teacher at the local *schul.* You have a reputation to think about." He slapped the palm of his hand on the flat arm of the rocker. "I can't have this behavior of yours continue."

"But I don't love Isaiah."

"You will grow to love him in time."

She shook her head so hard she felt the prayer *kapp* loosen. Fighting back tears, she straightened her *kapp*. "I can't do as you ask." Not when her heart belonged to someone else.

"Sadie! I'll not have you disobeying me!"

Sucking in a breath, her mind worked to find another way to convince her *daed* that this was not the right choice for her. Isaiah Troyer could never be her Amish man.

"I'm going to speak to him tomorrow," her *vader* warned.

She covered her mouth with one hand, pushing back the sob that threatened to escape. Her stomach roiled as her heart pounded inside her chest. This couldn't be happening, not when she and Levi were so close to... *Close to what?* she wondered. She let her eyelids drop, saying a silent prayer that her *daed* would give her more time. Sadie believed with all her heart and soul that Levi had been sent here not to help out Jacob but to find her.

Behind her, she heard the creak of the screen door.

Hoping to sway her *vader* once more, Sadie said, "I need more time."

"Nee."

"Wait!"

They both jumped at the sound of her sister's voice. Sara flew out onto the porch like a dog was nipping at her heels.

"Sadie isn't the right Fischer *dochder* for Isaiah," she blurted out. She stood in front of them, wringing her hands together. "I am."

"What is this nonsense?" their *vader* bellowed.

Sadie jumped up off the bench to stand with her sister, the life nearly scared right out of her. "Sara, what are you talking about?" Though thrilled her sister had intervened, Sadie worried that she might have gotten them both into more trouble than they were already in.

"Sadie isn't the one for Isaiah." Sara flung back her shoulders and speared their *vader* with a confident look. "I am."

Her *vader* narrowed his eyes. "You better explain yourself, Sara."

"Isaiah and I hit it off at the picnic. *Daed*, I've had feelings for him for a long time."

This admission made sense to Sadie, who'd been seeing the signs of Sara's affection toward Isaiah for months now. She recalled that Sara had been the one upset when the special dinner had to be canceled due to the storm. And Sara had been the one to put on her special dress the day of the picnic. And Sara had been the one to talk to Isaiah after church services.

Silence descended as the sisters collectively held their breath waiting for the final decision.

Their *vader* stood and walked to the far end of the porch. Placing both hands flat on the railing, he bowed his head. Sadie took hold of Sara's hand, giving it a squeeze. Even their *mamm* had come to stand in the doorway.

Sadie let out a nervous sigh. He was taking too long.

Finally, he turned to face them. "I will speak to Isaiah about you, Sara."

Sara broke away from Sadie, running to give their *vader* a hug. *"Danke!"*

Then she stepped to the side so their *vader* could deliver Sadie's fate.

"I know you think you have feelings for Levi Byler."

She didn't think it. She knew she'd fallen in love with the man.

"This should come as no surprise to you,

Sadie. News like this travels fast in close-knit communities. Before you ask me, I think you know why I've wanted this for you and Isaiah. I know very little about Levi, other than he is Jacob's cousin and appears to be a good worker."

"Jacob has officially offered him a partnership." Sadie thought this bit of news might help her *vader* to see that Levi was not simply passing through Miller's Crossing. There was a good chance he might settle here.

"Again, I will remind you that you have a reputation to uphold."

"I understand." Sadie knew she'd just been given her last chance to find her true love.

Chapter Fifteen

Sadie got to work early the next morning, her mind filled with yesterday's conversations with both her *vader* and Levi. She couldn't help thinking they all wanted the same outcome. Being a woman of faith, she knew the Lord had plans. The words of her *grossmudder* Fischer popped into her head.

For faith to prosper, it must experience impossible situations.

Sadie let out a morose laugh. Her love for Levi had certainly brought her an impossible situation. But she knew as sure as the sun would rise and set each day, her faith was as solid as a rock. And just as strong as her faith in the Lord, she'd faith that she and Levi would find their way. The signs had been there yesterday when she could see his concern for her after she'd learned about his offer. At first, she'd felt betrayed that he hadn't told her, then she reminded herself that Levi assumed they were finished.

She knew different.

Glancing out a window of the schoolhouse, she saw the *kinder* coming down the road. It was a sight that never got old. They came in groups of three and four, filtering out from their family's houses. The little girls wearing their blue *schlupp schotzli* over their dresses. Siblings and cousins helping one another to stay safe on the shared road. As soon as they hit the schoolyard, they ran across the grass and in through the basement entrance. All except for Mica. He straggled behind his group, scuffing his shoes through the tufts of grass.

Sadie hurried downstairs to the coatroom. "*Gute mariye*, everyone!"

Here and there, the children responded with their own, *"Gute mariye."*

She kept watch over the tops of their heads, until she saw Mica join them. "Everyone, let's put your lunches in your cubbies and then settle at your desks, please."

Mica avoided making eye contact with her, which Sadie didn't like.

They filed upstairs in order of youngest to

oldest. Each student took their seat and Sadie had them read aloud the morning Bible verse, then begin working on their math lessons.

The morning passed without incident. At eleven o'clock, she sent one of the older girls down to start the oven to warm the hot lunches. By noon everyone had eaten and was ready to go outside to play.

Mica had never been far from her sight. She noticed again that he didn't seem to want to read from his book. Though she did not like to stress it, obedience was one of the things they practiced here at the school. For the most part, her students behaved. Very rarely had she had to call upon a parent to come in, and heaven forbid, she'd never had to have the school board intervene on her behalf when it came to matters concerning parents and their children.

Still, her concern for Mica was growing.

"Mica, could you stop by my desk after you're done with your lunch, please?"

"Yes, Miss Sadie."

It pained her to see his mouth downturned. Sadie couldn't imagine what had gotten into him. Last year he'd been one of her best students. She didn't understand what had changed. She needed to get to the bottom of this and quickly.

She asked Mary Ellen and one of the other older girls to chaperone recess time. At twelve thirty on the dot, Mica arrived at her desk.

"Did you have a *gut* lunch?" she asked.

"Peanut butter and jelly, again." He rested his elbow on her desk, giving her a forlorn expression.

"I take it you don't like peanut butter and jelly?"

"It's okay. Not my favorite."

"I see. Now, tell me about last night's assignment. Did you get one of your parents to help with your reading?"

He shook his head.

"Why not?"

"They had chores to do."

"What about one of your older *bruders* or sisters?" Two of Mica's siblings had graduated last year, so Sadie knew they could help.

"Nee."

Bringing herself down to his eye-level, she reached across her desk and laid her hand gently on his arm. "Mica, can you tell me why you don't want to ask for help when you're at home?"

Again, he shook his head. She decided to try another tactic.

"How about you and I spend ten minutes during each recess working on your reading until you've caught up?"

"I can't do that either."

Sadie could almost feel his pain. Whatever was bothering him and keeping him from reading had to be pretty serious. "Mica? I need you to explain this to me."

"I can't do that."

His answer caused her to sit back in her chair. She watched him struggling and could tell he wanted to share his problem with her. Was he afraid of something at home? She prayed not.

An idea came upon her. "How about this. I'll read the pages from yesterday and you can follow along with me. Does that sound like a *gut* plan?" When he didn't respond, she added, "We have a test coming up on Friday, and it's going to have questions from these chapters. I know you want to do well."

His head moved up and down without looking up at her.

Satisfied that she had gotten through to him, Sadie asked him to bring his book up to her. Glancing at the clock, she saw there were fifteen minutes left of playtime. Mica would have to miss being outdoors with the other students today. Sadie felt bad about that, but it was important he kept pace with the others in his group.

While he got the book, she pulled another chair alongside hers. He sat down next to her and handed her the book. Sadie opened to the chapter he should have read and began reading to him. Every once in a while, she'd glance over to see if he were following along. At one point she paused. It seemed as if he were having problems seeing the words. Mica was leaning in close, squinting at the page.

Sadie nibbled her lower lip in thought.

The outside bell began to clang, signaling recess had come to an end. She would have to thank the girls for being so punctual with the time. Closing the book, she patted Mica on the shoulder. "Are you liking the book so far?"

He perked up a bit at her question. "I like when the boy tries to teach his sister how to fish."

Joy filled her heart. That was really *gut* to hear. It meant Mica had been paying attention even though he appeared to have trouble seeing the words. But she couldn't read to him every day. If her suspicions were correct, Mica was having trouble with his sight. She would send another note home and this time make him promise to show his parents.

The rest of the day flew by with ease. Sadie followed the routine, passing the trash can around the room for each student to toss out any papers they didn't need, and then escorted them to the coatroom, bidding them all a *gut* evening. She packed up and went home.

The next day dawned to begin the routine all over again, with Sadie arriving at the schoolhouse an hour before the *kinder*.

Judging from the buggy parked in front of the school, Sadie assumed Mica's parents had read her note. *Gut.* The sooner they figured out his problem, the quicker they could resolve it.

She noticed a familiar wagon parked out back. Levi must be doing some final touches on the shed.

Pushing her bike to the side of the building, she gathered the lesson plans she'd brought home last night and headed inside. The Kings were sitting in two chairs facing her desk. Sadie paused, gathering her thoughts, preparing to greet them.

"It's about time you arrived!" Robert King

turned to face her and stood behind his wife's chair.

From the doorway, Sadie said, "Mr. and Mrs. King. I didn't expect you."

Robert's *bruder* Amos owned the stationery store. Sadie realized they were quite different. Amos had always been kind to her, but she'd never gotten the feeling Robert was the same.

"Well, you should have after that note you sent home with Mica yesterday!" Robert's voice boomed through the room.

Calm. She needed to remain calm. Part of her job was to act on behalf of her students. She had to keep Mica's needs at the forefront. Bringing her papers with her, Sadie walked down the middle aisle. She rounded her desk and carefully set her things down. Then, raising her eyes, she faced Robert and Elenore King.

"What's this nonsense about him having problems reading?"

Sadie knew she had to tread lightly because Robert King sat on the school board. But that did not mean she wouldn't fight just as hard for Mica. As a matter of fact, Robert's stature made her want to dig in her heels to prove to him that she could handle this problem.

"Robert, Elenore. I noticed a few days ago that Mica seemed to have lost interest in doing his reading assignments."

"I'll speak to him about listening to you," Robert said.

"It's more than not listening. That's not it."

She decided it best not to mention Mica's complaint of the headache just yet. Sadie was quite certain Mica had told her that so she wouldn't push him to read in front of the class. She kept the part about the first note to herself, as well. If she needed extra leverage to convince the Kings to help him, she would tell them about the headache.

Sadie continued, "Yesterday I had him stay inside during recess to work with me. I decided to read out loud to him."

"I don't want you coddling my *sohn*," Robert admonished.

"I'm not doing that. I'm doing my job, trying to help him."

"His mother can help him."

"Robert, with all due respect, I believe that Mica's problem isn't that he can't read. It's that he's having struggles with his vision."

"What are you talking about?"

"I noticed that while he was following along, he had to lean in close to the page and then I saw him squinting. I think he needs to have his vision checked."

"You are no *doktor*! You are a teacher. Your job is to teach!"

"Robert!" Elenore put her arm on her husband's arm, stilling him. "Sadie has Mica's best interest at heart, I'm sure."

Pushing her hand away, he scolded, "Be quiet, Elenore." Continuing, he admonished Sadie, "You would do well to remember that you are still on probation here. Even if last year went fine, the school board hasn't ended their search for a new teacher."

Sadie stood there in shocked silence. She'd done nothing to deserve this kind of censure.

From outside the building, Levi heard what sounded like a male voice, raised in anger. Setting down the frame for the window box he'd been working on, he hurried to the schoolhouse.

Entering through the front door, he made his way to the threshold, just in time to hear a man say, "Perhaps it's not Mica's problem with his vision but the way you are teaching him."

Stunned, Levi walked into the classroom to see Sadie standing behind her desk visibly shaken. Her face ashen. It took every effort not to sprint over to the desk, take hold of the man at her desk and toss him outside. Coming to her defense seemed like the natural thing to do.

"Sadie Fischer is a *gut* teacher and you should consider yourself very fortunate to have her."

Sadie looked up, surprise registering on her face when she saw him standing there. She hadn't heard him come in.

The man glared at him. Levi immediately recognized Mica's *vader*. They'd met briefly after the storm. He wondered if the man remembered him. As the two of them stared at each other, Levi saw the anger simmering in Robert. The man's dark eyes narrowed, and his hands clenched at his side. Levi wondered why Robert didn't understand that Sadie only wanted the best for each and every one of her students, and Mica was no different.

Finally, Robert spoke. "I'm fairly certain you have no *kinder* in this school?"

"I do not."

"Then you have no business speaking here."

Levi stood there, weighing his options. He could apologize, or he could go back outside.

Or he could strengthen Sadie's defense, not that he thought for one minute she couldn't defend herself.

"Miss Sadie does a fine job of seeing to the needs of her students."

"I imagine you know this because of all the time you've been spending here."

This was exactly why he'd told Sadie there couldn't be more between them. As long as he was around here, and they were alone working together, there would continue to be problems for her. Levi hadn't come to Miller's Crossing to find love. He'd come to rebuild his life, as a single man. Even though there had never been anything untoward between them, he knew in their community appearances were everything.

"As you know, I've been working with her since the storm blew through. As a matter of fact, your *sohn* Mica has been one of our helpers. He did a fine job with the painting and helping me build the new shed. You should be right proud of him."

Robert's ire over the reading issue seemed to soften. "*Danke.* I'm surprised he stayed focused long enough to get any work done."

"The painting he seemed to take to, but the

work on the shed, not so much." Levi chuckled, hoping to break the tension in the room.

"He likes to horse around when he's outside." Robert swung his gaze back to Sadie.

"Robert, Elenore, I only want what's best for Mica," Sadie began. "As I'm sure you both do. Could you at least think about getting his eyes examined? If there is an issue, I imagine that soon it will carry over to other parts of his life. He's already complaining about headaches."

Elenore took hold of her husband's hand. "Please, Robert. We can at least think about what Sadie is saying."

"We'll discuss this at home." He stood up and then, nodding to Levi, said, "I'd like a word with you, outside."

Sadie's eyebrows rose.

Levi waited for Robert to join him and then took him down the stairs and out the basement door into the morning sunshine. Turning to face Mica's *daed*, he planted his feet about a foot apart, folded his arms across his chest and waited.

Robert's beard skimmed the top of his chest, and his gray hair reached almost to his shoulders. The man stood a good three inches taller than Levi. But even the steel gaze bearing down on him didn't intimidate him.

"Levi, I'm not one to beat around the bush, so I'll get right to the point of the matter. There's been gossip about you and Sadie Fischer. Part of my job on the school committee is to make sure the reputation of the teacher is a *gut* one, beyond reproach."

"I understand. My time with Sadie has been innocent. You can trust my word on that."

"You've been here working with her. Others saw you with her at the picnic. There may have been other times I've not been made aware of."

Levi felt his hackles raise. There had never been anything inappropriate between him and Sadie. He did not take these hints of accusation lightly. Moreover, he would never do anything to jeopardize her teaching job. Still, he found himself not liking the feeling Robert gave him. *Ja*, he knew how closely the Amish guarded their *dochders* and how many *vaders* worked hard to make the best arrangements for the good of the family. Sadie's *vader* hadn't been any different. But Levi had done nothing wrong.

This conversation left him with a sour taste in his mouth.

"I know Sadie understands this," Robert went on, "but I want to be certain that you do, too. It does not matter to me the work you've done to help out. And even though you are a relation to Jacob, you're a stranger here."

Levi continued to hold his stance even though he felt as if he'd been sucker punched.

Robert left him standing in the shadow of the shed, and Levi watched him walk back into the schoolhouse. Only when Robert was out of sight did he let his hands fall to his side. He spun around, and his eyes fell on the window boxes. His latest surprise for Sadie. Why did he keep torturing himself when he knew he wasn't going to accept Jacob's offer of the partnership?

How could he? He'd be living near Sadie. And Levi simply couldn't trust his heart or his feelings again. The pain Anne had wrought had left him deeply wounded. And even though some of those wounds had begun to heal, Levi still didn't think he could trust himself to make the right choice. This encounter with Robert King only reinforced the reasons why Levi couldn't stay in Miller's

Crossing and why he wasn't the right man for Sadie.

In all the weeks he'd been working side by side with her, he'd seen how she loved her *kinder*. Her days were devoted to making their lives better. He wouldn't be the one to destroy her happiness. He didn't want to rush headlong into another relationship.

Levi didn't know how to fix things.

He felt the ache growing inside him. He just wanted to do his work. Lord knows, he hadn't come here planning on falling in love. And yet that was exactly what had happened.

Pushing aside the pain and despair, Levi knew that the time had come for him to give Jacob an answer to his offer. But first he would finish what he started.

Picking up a two-by-eight plank, he placed it on the sawhorses, measured and cut the plank to size, two inches longer than the front of the windows. He did that one more time, and then, laying the tape measure along the wood, he measured out six inches in length and proceeded to cut four of those.

As the morning wore on, the *kinder*'s voices floated through the open window. Every once in a while, he heard the sweet sound of Sadie's voice either giving instruction or offering encouragement. When he heard the singing, he stopped his work to listen. The song, a familiar one, reminded him of home and family and of his love for the Lord. The hymn called to mind all the good that life could bring a person.

He didn't want to wallow. Shaking himself out of the doldrums, he hammered the pieces of wood into place until they resembled two long boxes. Then he hung one box beneath each window. Going to his wagon, he hefted the bag of potting soil onto his shoulder and brought it over to the work area. He filled both boxes with dirt, then gathered the pots of mums from his wagon.

He'd been first in line at Troyer's nursery this morning so he could pick out the prettiest plants. He'd chosen purple, yellow and white petunias.

Their blooms danced in the breeze. The purple reminded him of the way Sadie's eyes changed color depending on her mood. The pots of white mums brought to mind her strength, and the yellow ones made him think of how she embraced whatever came her way. And he'd not forgotten yellow was her favorite color.

Levi hoped she would like this final gift.

He placed one plant of each color in the window boxes. Patting the soil into place, Levi listened to the sounds of the *kinder* and realized he would miss them, almost as much as he would miss Sadie. Stepping back, he brushed his hands together, letting the loose dirt fall. He gave one last look to his handiwork and, satisfied that he'd done his best, began packing up the wagon.

A selfish part of him wanted to stay so he could see the look on her face when she stepped outside to see these flowers.

He'd started to untie the horse from the hitching post when he realized he'd left his tool belt on the ground by the shed. He jogged back over, picked it up and turned to see the *kinder* streaming out the coatroom door.

"Mr. Byler! How are you?" Mica ran up to him.

Patting the boy on the head, Levi said, "I'm *gut*, and how about yourself?"

"I'm doing okay, I guess." His face took on a glum expression. "I'm having trouble with my reading, so Miss Sadie has been helping me."

"I see. Well, it's important to know how to read."

"I understand, but I'd rather be outside playing."

Levi imagined he did.

"Mica!" Sadie's voice carried over on a breeze.

Levi took his hand off Mica's head and watched Sadie come out of the coatroom into the brilliant day. She raised a hand to shield her eyes from the sunlight. He saw her scan the area, looking for Mica.

Mica's *vader*'s words came back to Levi. As long as he remained here, her reputation could be at stake.

The Amish rules of courtship were strict. Levi knew them well. Sadie's *vader* had chosen for her. Watching her, he wondered what would happen if he decided to stay.

"I'm over here, Miss Sadie, talking to Mr. Levi."

Mica ran past her as she walked toward the shed, then Sadie stopped dead in her tracks.

Chapter Sixteen

"Wow!" she breathed out.

She stared at the beautiful petunias in the planter boxes hanging beneath each window on the front of the shed. She placed her hand on her heart. Levi's gesture was so thoughtful it brought tears of happiness. He'd been so stubborn about wanting to even give her the windows and now he'd gone and done this.

It almost made up for the earlier upset between him and Mica's *vader.* Almost. But she'd get back to that in a minute. First, she had to get a closer look at these flowers.

She couldn't keep the grin off her face as she went over to inspect the boxes. Up close the plants were even prettier. The vibrant purples along with the clean-white and sunshine-yellow flowers made her heart sing. She wondered how Levi had known to pick out her favorite colors.

She spun around to tell him how grateful she was for this gift. "Levi. *Danke. Danke* so much! You don't know how much joy this will bring the *kinder.* In the spring we can put different flowers in these boxes. And I know you didn't think any of my ideas were worth keeping in the beginning. But I can tell from the look on your..." She had to stop herself from blurting out *handsome face.*

Calming down, she said, "I can tell from the look on your face that you think these boxes and the windows look wonderful."

"I think you look wonderful."

The words had come out so softly that she thought she might have imagined them.

Her heart skipped a beat. Levi had paid her a compliment. The first one since they'd known each other. Though she tried not to get her hopes up, she wondered if this meant he wanted to move forward in their relationship. She dared not speak.

"I'm glad you like the flower boxes," he said a little louder. "And, *ja,* you were right. The windows are a *gut* fit."

Sadie didn't like his brusque new tone.

Levi took a step away from her. As sure as

a dark rain cloud came over the horizon to spoil an otherwise perfect day, she watched Levi's mood shift. Sadie didn't understand what was happening.

"Well, I'm done here," he said. "I'd best be getting back over to Jacob's shop."

"Wait!" Sadie started after him. She needed to find out what Robert had spoken to him about.

Levi stopped and turned to look at her. Sadie didn't like what she saw, not one little bit. It appeared that a wall had gone up around him, worse than all those times before when she'd tried to break through to him. And when she'd so recently called him out on not telling her about the partnership offer.

Plunging ahead, she said, "I suppose I should thank you for intervening with Mica's *vader.* Honestly, I could have handled the man by myself. Dealing with distressed parents is part of my job."

His chin came up at her words. "Robert King had no business raising his voice to you."

"I agree. But he thought I wanted to tell him how to parent his *sohn.* Which I did not." Lowering her voice, so as not to have the *kinder* overhear, she confided, "I believe

Mica is having trouble with his vision. He needs to see an eye *doktor.* I'm afraid Robert doesn't seem to agree with my assessment."

"That's not all he doesn't agree with."

"What are you talking about?" Sadie had a terrible feeling this had something to do with Levi.

Putting up his hand, he shook his head. "I can't talk about this."

"*Ja*, I think you need to. Tell me what Robert said to you."

"*Nee.* It will only cause trouble."

"Levi, if you are worried that I can't handle the situation, you'd be wrong. Just like when you walked in on my meeting earlier. You were wrong to interrupt. I didn't need your help. Although I appreciate your kind words on my behalf, I had the situation under control."

He leaned against the wagon. Shaking his head, he pointed a finger at her. "I don't think you did. Robert King was upset and he was standing over you and his wife, trying to intimidate you. *Es dutt mir leed*, Sadie, but I'm glad I came into the classroom when I did."

Sadie's frustration with him boiled over. The situation with this man had been tenuous for days, ever since he'd told he couldn't be the one for her. Sadie knew better. She could also tell that he was in no mind to listen to reason but that still didn't stop her from voicing her opinion.

"Levi, you can't have this both ways. You can't push me away one minute and then want to protect me the next. You can't leave me with this wonderful gift—" pausing, she looked at the window boxes "—and not think that I wouldn't see it as a sign of your affection."

They seemed to be at an impasse. Sadie fought back the heartache. This man, the only one she could ever love, stood here in his blue chambray work shirt, with his straw hat covering his light brown hair, leaning against the wagon, rubbing his hand down his face. She knew he wanted to wipe away his frustration. She clasped her hands together, not knowing what else to do. She felt her faith wavering.

Finally, Levi said, "I didn't want to tell you what Robert said. But I don't see any other way to protect you, to protect your job. He warned me to stay away from you. He said your reputation is at stake."

She started to tell him that was just Robert spewing nonsense when she heard one of the *kinder*'s cries. Her gaze quickly scanned the schoolyard to see who needed her.

Little Beth sat on the ground in front of the swing set, holding her right knee.

Without a thought, Sadie rushed over and kneeled in front of the girl. "Beth, *bischt all-recht*?"

Beth let out a sob as tears streamed down her face. "I fell off the swing," she wailed.

"There, there. Let me take a look." Sadie pushed Beth's *schlupp schotzli* off her knee and saw where her stockings had torn. Near as she could tell, this was nothing more than a scrape. But to be on the safe side, she would take Beth inside to clean it and put on a Band-Aid.

"Do you think you can walk?"

Beth's lower lip trembled. "I don't think so. I think it might be broken."

"Beth, I can assure you your knee is not broken. Now, come on and try to stand up," Sadie coaxed.

Doing as she was told, the child started to stand, and then let out a shout. Sadie knew the scrape wasn't serious. Still, she pushed herself off the ground, preparing to gather Beth in her arms to carry her inside. But before she could move, she felt a hand on her shoulder.

"Let me help." Levi's shadow covered them.

Sadie stood up the rest of the way, allowing

him to move past her to scoop Beth up off the ground as if she were light as a feather. Levi cradled her in his arms as Sadie ran ahead to get the coatroom door opened.

"I've got a first-aid kit over by the sink." Sadie led them to the small kitchenette.

Levi sat Beth on the countertop.

"*Danke*, Mr. Levi." Beth batted her tear-soaked lashes at him.

Sadie thought her heart would melt at the sweet look on that little girl's face, so she could only imagine what Levi had to be thinking. He turned to her and Sadie sighed over the fact that he still appeared to be carrying that dark cloud with him.

"I'll leave this to you," he said in a brusque tone.

Sadie recognized that their situation would have to wait. Offering him her thanks, she gave her attention to Beth. For the first time since she'd met Levi and fallen in love with him, Sadie felt her resolve cracking.

Nee. She prayed for patience and strength. *I have to stay strong.*

As Levi made his way back to the shed company, he tried not to dwell on the situation with Sadie. But how could he not? At every twist and turn, no matter how hard he tried to keep them at bay, thoughts of her floated through his mind.

And it didn't help that the ride back to Jacob's seemed to take forever. The road was crowded today, with cars and eighteen-wheelers everywhere. With the fall season coming, the tourists were out and about earlier in the week. Here in Miller's Crossing, the leaves were just beginning to turn colors, the green leaves tinged with oranges and reds. A part of him wished he'd be here to see the colors at their peak.

He waited for the traffic to clear at the intersection of Clymer Hill Road and Route Ten. When it came his turn, he turned right onto Clymer Hill.

The horse slowed as it started the ascent up the long hill. The wagon rattled along, cresting at the rise where the church stood. He remembered the day he'd first met Sadie. What a sight she'd been stuck in the mudhole. From the top of her head to the tips of her toes, she'd been a soggy mess. Even then he'd been struck by her presence and her personality.

A buggy careening around the corner at the bottom of the hill interrupted his musings.

"What on earth? Hey!" He gave a shout as

the buggy came full speed up the hill. "Hey! *Was iss letz* with you! Slow down!"

The buggy pulled to a halt beside him. Levi immediately recognized one of the workers from the shop.

Mark Miller barely got the words out. "Levi! I'm so glad I found you! There's been an accident. You must come quickly!"

"Slow down. Tell me what's happened."

"Jacob took a fall outside his house. Rachel said he needed to go to the hospital."

Concern filled Levi. He prayed his friend's injuries were not serious. "All right." Seeing the young man was upset, Levi asked, "Did Rachel call for an ambulance?"

"*Nee.* Jacob insisted they call one of the neighbors. They came by and drove him away. I think he injured his arm."

"Okay, let's get back to the house."

Levi waited for the lad to turn around in the church parking lot, and then led the way back to Rachel and Jacob's. He saw some of the workers standing around in a circle outside the shop. Their heads were bowed, and Jacob knew they were praying for their boss. He grew worried. If they had all stayed, then Jacob's condition must be serious.

Leaving the horse with some water and a bit of grain, he walked across the lot to join them.

"Levi. *Gut* you came back when you did. Jacob took a tumble down the steps coming out of his house. Rachel thinks he might have broken something."

"Did anyone else see what happened?"

"*Nee*. Most of us were inside."

"How long do you think they've been gone?" he asked.

"About half an hour."

That was too soon for any news. Levi looked at the men, who were all watching him. It took him a minute to realize they were waiting on some sort of instruction from him.

"I think it's best if we all go back to work," he said. "I'll go check to make sure Rachel didn't leave anything cooking on the stove. I'm sure she left in a hurry."

"*Ja*, she looked very upset."

The men made their way back inside the shop while Levi headed up the small incline to the house. He paused at the bottom of the porch steps. He could see multiple footprints where he guessed Jacob had fallen. He also saw the crack in the second step from the bottom. Not a *gut* thing. Skipping that step, he went on into the house.

Immediately, he could smell freshly baked bread and chicken. Hurrying through the great room, he saw two loaves of bread on a wire rack near the stove. And sure enough, simmering away on the back unit was a large black pot. Lifting the lid, he waited for the steam to clear, then peered inside. A whole chicken languished in the bubbling liquid along with celery, carrots and onions.

No doubt the beginning of the evening meal, and probably stock for later. He decided to turn it off. If he got busy outside, he didn't want to forget the pot and have the liquid cook off, scorching the chicken to the bottom. Better to be safe than sorry.

Now that he'd gotten the cooking under control, he turned his attention to fixing the step.

He went out the back door to the small outbuilding where Jacob stored his personal tools. He slid the door open, surprised to find everything neatly organized. The shovels, rakes and hoes were all hung neatly on the right side. He found a big red multi-drawer toolbox and opened a drawer marked Hammers. He picked up a medium-size one and selected a few large nails that would easily hold the repair.

Back at the porch, he tore the old step off the risers, then walked over to the scrap pile outside the shop to see if he could find something that could work as a replacement. After a bit of rummaging around, he managed to find a board that looked close enough in size. He hammered it into place, then tested the tread with his weight. This would suffice. With the job done, he returned everything back to its place in the outbuilding.

The sunlight angled through the branches of the maple trees circling the yard. Levi walked through the coolness of the shadows. He needed to check in on the workers. The end of the day was nearing, and they'd all be going home soon.

"Levi! We're wrapping up here."

He met Saul Yoder just inside the doorway. "Is there anything I need to be worried about on behalf of Jacob?"

"*Nee.* We're set with the biggest project, which is for Troyer's Nursery and Garden Center."

"*Gut.* When do you think that will be finished?"

"I'd say by the end of next week. Do you think Jacob will be out of work long?"

"I can't say until we see what his injuries are."

"For what it's worth, the others and I, well, we think you'd be a *gut* fit for Jacob's company."

Levi's eyes widened. He had no idea anyone else knew about the partnership offer.

"I can tell by the look on your face I spoke out of turn," Saul said. "I'm sorry. Nevertheless, we'd all be happy to have you join the company."

Levi decided to let the comment go. Saul had intended no harm. No one knew of his indecision when it came to accepting Jacob's offer. This was Levi's battle.

Saul and Levi made their way around the shop, checking to be sure each station had been shut down correctly and readied for the next day. He noticed a light on in the office. Like many other Amish businesses in the area, this one was powered by a combination of propane, generators and solar power. Bidding Saul good-night, Levi entered the office.

He saw the lamp on the desk and started to turn it off when his hand hit a stack of papers, sending them onto the floor. He bent down to pick them up and stopped when he saw a lawyer's letterhead on one of the papers. Knowing this was none of his business, he started to shuffle them in place. And that was when he saw his name.

Squinting, he mumbled, "What is this?"

Chapter Seventeen

He cast a quick look over his shoulder to make sure no one had seen him. This didn't make sense. Why was his name on a legal document? He stood from the floor and sat down with the paper in Jacob's chair. Going through his friend's legal papers made him feel like a criminal. But he had to see what Jacob had done.

Levi took his hat off and laid it on the desk next to some crisp white stationery. He ran his hands through his hair in frustration, and then, taking the plunge, he started to read through the document.

The top page appeared to be a cover letter. It stated the reason Jacob had contacted the attorney and detailed the scope of what Jacob would need done in order to secure a partner in the Herschberger Shed Company. One of the pages talked about the possibility of changing the name of the company to Herschberger and Byler.

As flattering as this idea was, Levi didn't understand why Jacob would go to all this trouble and not discuss this with him first. He'd seen enough. Putting the papers back in place, he turned the light off and went back up to the house to wait.

He took some leftover roast beef out of the refrigerator and made a sandwich. After pouring himself a glass of iced *kaffi*, he grabbed his plate and headed out to the front porch. While he ate, he wondered how Jacob was faring. And he mulled over this idea of the partnership. Clearly the employees didn't mind him coming on. And truth be told, the idea of finally settling down held some appeal. But could he stay here and not have contact with Sadie?

Once again, he wished he'd met her earlier in his life. Leaning back in the rocker, Levi pondered the situation. This partnership with Jacob would mean he'd leave his family permanently. He'd become a member of the Miller's Crossing church community. *Ja*, he'd see his *mamm* and *daed* on occasion, and writing letters to them helped them stay connected. He knew his parents always had his best interests at heart. They were as devastated as he had been over what had happened with Anne.

He finished the *kaffi* and sandwich, then set the plate on the table. Levi tipped his head back, closed his eyes and let the sounds of nature wash over him. Off in the distance he heard a hawk screeching and the frogs croaking in a nearby pond. Life could be *gut* here in Miller's Crossing.

He heard gravel crunching under tires and opened his eyes to see the beam of headlights sweeping across the driveway. Pushing up from the chair, he hurried off the porch.

Rachel was getting out of the back seat of a blue sedan. "Oh, Levi! I'm so glad you're here."

"How's Jacob?"

"Come and see for yourself." Rachel scurried to the passenger-side front seat.

Levi followed, anxious to see how his cousin had fared. He let out an *"ach"* when he saw Jacob's right arm in a cast and a sling.

While Rachel held the car door open, Levi helped Jacob out of the car as best he could. His friend seemed to be a bit wobbly on his feet. When Jacob swayed, Levi held on to his good arm. "Whoa. I've got you."

"Dan...ke."

Coming up behind them, Rachel advised, "He's been given a mild painkiller."

Levi nodded, taking care to guide Jacob up the porch stairs. "I fixed the step."

"*Danke! Danke*, Levi. That's the one that caused Jacob's fall," Rachel said, racing ahead of them to hold open the front door. "Take him into our bedroom. He needs to lie down and raise the arm up above his heart. The doctor said it will help keep the swelling down."

Again, she pushed her way ahead of the men, getting Jacob's side of the bed ready with extra pillows. Levi guided Jacob to sit on the bed.

"Ah." Jacob let out a relieved sigh. "I've had quite the time of it, I'm afraid. I noticed the step had cracked earlier today. I was actually coming out to fix it when I fell. Can you believe that?"

"*Ja*. These things happen," Levi answered as he helped him lie back in the bed.

"Jacob, I'm going to make you some toast," Rachel said. "The nurse said you have to take the medication with food. And how about some tea?" She tipped her head to one side, gazing down at her husband.

"*Ja*, that will be fine."

Thinking Jacob might need to rest, Levi started to follow Rachel out.

"Levi, wait. Let me have a word with you before Rachel comes back."

Levi paused at the foot of the bed, noticing the lines of fatigue around Jacob's eyes and the occasional grimace of pain on his face.

"I'm worried. The *doktor* said I fractured two bones in my wrist. One is what they called a hairline and the other is a bit more serious. They don't think I will need an operation to fix it, but the next few weeks will decide the course. I have to have this on for four to six weeks." he said, tapping on the hard cast. He started to give Levi a grin, but failed miserably.

"Look," Levi assured him, "I don't want you to worry about anything. You concentrate on resting and healing. It's getting late. I'll leave you to Rachel's care."

Softly, he closed the bedroom door behind him as he went to join Rachel in the kitchen.

"*Danke* for taking care of the pot, Levi," she said. "I completely forgot about it being on. Everything happened so fast. He was going down the steps one minute and the next he was on the ground calling out for me."

"He seems to be doing well and the *gut* news is he came back home without a stay in the hospital."

She nodded. "We were lucky that the urgent care could do everything. He needs to see a specialist in a few days. Those are all *gut* things. Did he tell you about the injury?"

"Ja."

"I'm not sure he told you everything. The nurse was very clear to me. He needs to keep that arm still. They want the fractures to heal well so they don't have to do an operation to fix them."

He saw the distress on her face and wanted to let her know that he would be here for them. "That makes sense. You know you both can count on me to help run things while Jacob heals."

"I'm glad you'll be here, is all."

The teakettle let out a shrill whistle. Rachel took it off the heat and went about fixing the tea and toast for her husband. "I know you can see to the running of the business while my Jacob recovers." Rachel put the teacup and saucer on a tray next to the plate of toast.

Remembering the papers he'd seen in the

office, Levi knew he couldn't leave, not under these circumstances. He would get back to the idea of the partnership when Jacob was feeling better. But for now, temporarily, he'd stay put. A *gut* man did not walk out on his family when they were in need.

"Lizzie and I have come up with a plan to get you and Levi together."

Sadie stared dumbfounded at her sister. Sara, who had been beaming like a ray of sunshine for days now, was sitting here giving her advice on matters of the heart. Ever since their *vader* had given his blessing on her courting Isaiah, she'd been walking around with a happiness that appeared to be never ending. Meanwhile, Sadie had been existing in limbo. But today Sara had invited their friend Lizzie over for afternoon tea when all Sadie wanted was to wallow in a bit of self-pity.

She picked at the needlepoint she'd brought out to the porch to work on. There might not be enough rose-colored thread to finish. The design was a simple one: *Love is the reason behind everything God does.* She'd planned on making this for herself, hoping to hang it in her own home one day. Now she would finish it and give it to her sister as a wedding gift.

Picking up the threaded needle, she poked it through the fabric, working on the letter *o* in *Love*.

"We're going to have a potluck dinner." Sara clapped her hands together in delight.

"Rachel wants us to come to her place," Lizzie added. "She said her refrigerator is overflowing with casseroles. Everyone who stops by to visit Jacob comes with a dish in hand. I stopped by yesterday to leave a loaf of my homemade banana bread."

"And I'm to come as the extra?" Sadie hated the bitterness in her voice. Her frustration with Levi boiled over.

Both Sara and Lizzie had stricken looks on their faces.

"Sadie, you listen to me," Sara demanded. "Levi will be there."

"You seem awfully sure of yourself, Sara."

"*Ja*, I am. He's staying there, for goodness' sake. This situation between the two of you has to be resolved. The dinner will be tomorrow."

Sadie's stomach churned. "Tomorrow."

"That's right," Lizzie said, exchanging glances with Sara.

This turn of events had Sadie nibbling on her lower lip. She knew that Levi wouldn't be happy with this setup.

She wanted to confess something to Sara and Lizzie but didn't quite know how to form the words. Finally, knowing that getting this off her mind would be better than keeping it inside, she said, "I believe something is holding Levi back. I'm not exactly sure what the problem might be, but something from his past is clearly troubling him and keeping him from moving on with his life."

"Have you spoken to him about this?" Sara asked.

"Sara, I have tried every which way to get him to open up to me. This burden he is carrying is great. He doesn't trust what I know is in his heart."

"Hmm." Lizzie sipped thoughtfully at her tea. "I know one thing for sure, Sadie. God's plans should never be questioned."

"Are you thinking I should let Levi go?" Sadie got choked up just thinking it.

"That is not what I'm saying at all. Do you remember how hard I fought my love for Paul?"

Sadie laughed. "*Ja.* You were being so stubborn."

"That I was. I didn't think any man could ever love a woman who looks like I do." Lizzie rubbed her hand over the scar on her face. "But I finally gave into what my heart was telling me and what Paul knew all along. We were meant to be together."

Sadie's friend had been through a lot. The death of her *bruder* in a tragic accident, when they were young *kinder*, had left her scarred inside and out. But Lizzie had persevered and found her true love.

Setting her glass down on the low table between them, Lizzie leaned over and patted Sadie on the knee. "You will get this figured out."

A restlessness filled her. Putting the needlepoint down on the table, she stood up, stretching her arms. Nothing she did these days seemed to erase the tension that had taken root between her shoulder blades. "I'm going to go into the village to see if Decker's has the thread I need."

"Do you want company?" Sara asked.

"*Nee.* A walk might do me some good. Maybe the time will clear my head." Sadie went inside to grab her wallet. She said goodbye to Sara and Lizzie, then headed out.

She did enjoy the walk and the fresh air.

By the time she arrived in Clymer, she had worked up a bit of a thirst. Going into the grocery store, she found the thread she needed in the home goods section and decided to treat herself to some root beer. She paid for the two items and stepped out onto the sidewalk.

"Yoo-hoo! Sadie!"

Chapter Eighteen

Elenore King came rushing up to her. "Oh, Sadie, I'm so glad I ran into you. I was across the street at the café."

"*Gute nammidaag*, Elenore."

"*Ja. Ja. Gute nammidaag* to you."

The woman seemed to be in a bit of distress. She was wringing her hands and could barely keep still. Sadie worried that something might have happened to Mica. "Elenore, *was iss letz*?"

Shaking her head, Elenore replied, "Nothing is wrong. At least I hope not."

This didn't sound *gut*. Sadie didn't think she could handle any more stress in her life. Clearly, this woman had something she wanted to tell her. Sadie thought asking about

Mica might get her to talking. "How is Mica doing with his reading?"

"That's one of the things I wanted to tell you about. First, let me apologize again for Robert's treatment of you the other day."

"There's no need for that."

"I think there is. You are a *gut* teacher. I think one of the best Miller's Crossing has had in a long time. Robert was having a bad day. And that's no excuse for his behavior."

"I understand."

"He's been busy with work and of course providing for our family. This problem with Mica came at a bad time is all," she explained. "But I want you to know I convinced him to let us take Mica to the eye *doktor*."

"Elenore! This is wonderful news!" Sadie knew that Mica's reading would be back on track soon.

"Mica's eyes are weak. He's going to be wearing glasses while he's in school and for doing his reading and homework."

Sadie realized it had taken great courage and strength for Elenore to convince her husband to let this happen. Though she never doubted that the man cared for his family, he was known to be strict with them.

"I'm so happy for Mica."

Elenore fidgeted with the drawstring on the bag she was carrying. Her gaze didn't quite meet Sadie's eyes as she said, "There's one more thing I need to tell you."

"What is it?"

"The school board is meeting tonight. They are going to be deciding on your position."

Elenore's words hit her hard. Sadie had known this day would come. She'd understood from the beginning that this job might be temporary. Still, the idea of her fate being in the hands of three members of her community worried her.

"*Danke* for letting me know."

"Willkomm," Elenore replied, and then went off, leaving Sadie standing near the intersection of Main Street and Route Ten.

She didn't know what to make of this news other than realizing she didn't want to leave the *kinder*.

The stoplight was on its third cycle of green, yellow, then red when she heard a very familiar voice say, "Are you going to stand here all day or are you crossing the street?"

She looked at Levi, blinking back tears.

"Sadie? Is something the matter?" He stepped toward her.

She backed away, blurting out, "The school board is meeting tonight."

"I see."

"They are going to be talking about me. Deciding *my* future." She poked herself in the chest. "What if I'm not the person they want to teach their *kinder*?"

"Sadie, I don't believe for one minute that they will let you go. Nor should you."

"Levi, Robert told me just last week that he'd be watching me closely. And I think he told you the same." She swallowed. "I took the job because I was looking for something to do to fill the time until I found…" She stopped talking.

Levi took a half step toward her and reached out a hand to her. But then, realizing they were in public where anyone could see them, he let the hand drop.

"Until you found what?"

"You know what I've been searching for."

He did.

"The *kinder* adore you." *I adore you.* "I've seen how they look up to you. And you bring such life into their lives. How can you think the school board won't see that?"

"I only know that my heart was in the wrong place when I began teaching last year.

My reasons for accepting the temporary position were selfish. I simply thought I could walk into that classroom, do my teaching and leave. I wanted to fill this void in my life. And you know what? The *kinder* do fill my life. I love to see the expressions on their faces when they solve a problem. And one of my older students, Mary Ellen, why, she's growing up so fast and is a *gut* helper to me. Every night I go home thinking about the next day and all the new things we'll learn together."

She paused, as if remembering they were having this conversation in a very public place. She put her shoulders back and tilted her chin up to give him one of the fiercest looks he'd ever seen. "I can't lose them."

He almost cracked a smile, thinking there was the woman he loved. Levi longed to take her in his arms, to give her the comfort she so desperately needed. But he couldn't. He had decisions of his own to make. And only when he settled things in his own life would he be able to open his heart to her. A woman who richly deserved so much more than he could ever give her.

Tipping his hat back, he asked, "Will I see you tomorrow at Rachel and Jacob's?"

She seemed surprised by his question. "You know about the potluck?"

He nodded. Why wouldn't he know about the plans Rachel had made with Lizzie? "Rachel is very excited about having company. She's been so busy worrying over her husband that she's making herself crazy."

"But you've been there to help."

It wasn't a question but he answered anyway. *"Ja."*

"Gut."

Levi could almost see her mind wandering back to her problem. He hoped the board wouldn't use his friendship with her against her when making their decision. That wouldn't be fair. As far as he was concerned, they'd done nothing inappropriate.

"Listen, whatever happens at this meeting tonight, you've got your friends and family who will support you no matter what," he said.

"I know. I wish I could be there at the meeting. I'm not the most patient person."

He winked at her. She didn't need to remind him of that.

She gave him a half smile. "I guess I need to be getting back home. I'll see you tomorrow."

He wanted to offer her a ride but knew

she'd turn him down. He watched her walk off, praying tomorrow would bring the answers she'd been hoping for. As for himself, he knew the time had come to settle things concerning the partnership.

He got back to the shop and was surprised to find Jacob sitting behind the desk in the office.

"So, you've finally grown tired of being cooped up?" Levi asked.

"As much as I love her, my wife has been driving me crazy with all of her coddling," Jacob admitted. "I know she's worried, but the trip to the specialist went better than we could have hoped."

"Is the cast coming off anytime soon?"

"*Nee.* Three more weeks, I'm afraid. But the bone is healing."

"I'm glad. You don't seem to be in as much pain either."

"I'm not. And that's a *gut* thing and another reason I want to get back out here—" Jacob nodded toward the shop area "—to work."

"You've got a lot of really dependable employees. They were all praying for you to have a speedy recovery."

"*Ja*, they are *gut* men. If we expand, I'll

have to go outside of Miller's Crossing to find helpers. Would you be okay with that?"

The *we* part of his statement wasn't lost on Levi. His friend had been patient with him long enough. Jacob slid the contract Levi had found a week ago across the desk to him.

"I've had an attorney work on some papers. Do you want to take a look at them?"

Sitting down, Levi crossed one leg, resting the heel of his boot across the other knee. He took his time, tempering his words. "I already saw these papers."

Jacob raised an eyebrow.

"I came out here the day you fell to close up the shop, and noticed a light on in the office. When I came in, I found the documents."

"I'm assuming you looked through them."

Levi would never hold back the truth from his cousin. "I saw my name and looked at a few of the top pages."

Resting his good arm on top of the desk, Jacob studied him. Levi toyed with the cuff on the bottom of his pant leg.

"Levi, what do you think of what you've seen so far?" Jacob asked at last.

"I think it seems like a fair deal. But I'm wondering why you would want to add someone else's name to the business. The change would incur another expense. You'd have to change your branding."

"I think it's the right thing to do. My attorney advised waiting to see how a new partnership would work out before putting through that particular paperwork." Jacob leaned in, pushing the contract almost to the edge of the desk.

Levi chuckled. The man was determined. He grabbed the contract before it landed on the floor and sat back in his chair, reading through each page.

Jacob wanted a very nominal buy-in. Levi suspected it was because Jacob wanted Levi to bring something to the table other than financial strength. He got to the part about the company name change. His name looked *gut* on paper.

Still, he worried Jacob was being too generous. If this arrangement did not work out, then he'd be left with a company that bore someone else's name. The impact of the decision struck him. If he stayed here in Miller's Crossing, this would become his home. If he gave in to his feelings for Sadie, there would be no turning back.

And would either of these choices be so bad?

"I hear we're having company for dinner tomorrow night. I think the women have something planned." Jacob's voice broke the silence.

Levi shot a glance at him, thinking back on the conversation he'd had with Sadie earlier. She'd had a funny look on her face when they talked about the dinner. He began to grow suspicious.

"I don't know about your theory," he said. "I think they wanted to have a gathering is all."

Jacob shrugged. "If you say so. I still think they're up to something. You about done with your reading?"

"Give me another minute." Levi wanted to look over the last page one more time. The page with the signature line.

Jacob slid his pen across the desk.

"Sadie, did you start the bratwurst?" Sara asked.

"I'm not sure why you want to bring this. Didn't Rachel already say she has a lot of food?"

"Yes. But I think Isaiah might like it."

"Then why aren't you the one making the dish? I'm busy baking my cookies," Sadie snapped.

The day had been wearing on and still there was no word of the school board's decision. But she hadn't meant to take her frustrations out on her sister.

"Sadie! You apologize to your sister right this instant," their *mamm* ordered. Turning around from the sink, she speared Sadie with a look she hadn't seen since she was a *kinder.*

"Es dutt mir leed, Sara. Forgive me, please." Wiping her hands on a towel, she added, "I don't know what's gotten into me."

"This is so unlike you, Sadie," her *mamm* added.

"Es dutt mir leed, Mamm." Dropping the towel on the counter, Sadie ran out of the kitchen and onto the front porch.

The pressure of waiting for the news was too much for her. So much of her life hung on the edge. Her job. Her relationship with Levi. Whether or not Levi would choose to become a partner and stay in Miller's Crossing. She leaned against a post at the top of the steps, trying to calm her nerves. But the thoughts kept coming. She feared her life would never hold the happiness she sought. She thought about her encounter with Levi yesterday.

Something about him had changed. She couldn't put her finger on exactly what, but he hadn't pushed her away. *Nee*. If anything, she'd felt closer to him.

She saw her *vader* coming up the pathway from the barn.

"*Dochder*, I have a note for you."

Sadie ran down the steps to meet him. This could be the news she was waiting for. With a shaky hand, she took the envelope he held out to her and saw her name in neat block lettering.

"Is this something important?" her *vader* asked.

"*Ja.*" Sadie's nerves were rattling so much she barely got the word out.

A million thoughts ran through her mind. If the school board was keeping her, surely they would have sent someone by to tell her in person. On the other hand, if they were going to let her go, she imagined Robert King might have taken great pleasure in delivering that news himself. She didn't know what to do.

And then a thought hit her. As sure as the sun rose and set, there was only one person she wanted with her when she opened this envelope.

She left her *vader* and ran back inside the house. "Sara, do you have everything ready to go?"

"Sadie, what's gotten into you now?" her *mamm* asked.

"Nothing. And everything." Sadie gave her *mamm* a hug, then picked up the red cookie tin with her snickerdoodles.

Sara was just putting the foil on the bratwurst. "Are we leaving? Isaiah isn't here yet. Did you forget he's driving us?"

Sadie had forgotten. "Okay, let's wait for him at the top of the driveway."

"Sadie!"

"Come on, hurry up!" She tugged her sister by the arm toward the door.

She needed to get to Levi.

Chapter Nineteen

Levi was helping Rachel put the dishes out on the picnic table in the side yard. She'd told him evenings like this were not to be wasted eating indoors. He set a dish of baked chicken in the middle of the table, along with the green bean casserole, baked macaroni and cheese, another pasta dish and a large tossed salad. The neighbors had been generous with their offerings during Jacob's recovery. And he couldn't even begin to think about the number of pies and cakes that filled the second shelf of the refrigerator.

Speaking of desserts, he hoped Sadie might bring her blue-ribbon snickerdoodles. Levi hoped she'd have good news, too.

He'd been thinking about her all day long. He prayed the school board had made the right decision, because he had a bit of his own news to share with her.

Moving to the other side of the table, he fixed the thin cushion over the bench. Rachel had insisted they use them. While the menfolk didn't mind sitting on hard benches, she assured him the ladies preferred a bit more comfort.

A buggy pulled up in front of the house, and Levi stood taller, waiting for Sadie to get out. Surprise ricocheted through him when he saw Isaiah Troyer climbing down from the front seat.

How could Sadie do this to him? Was this some sort of bad joke that life had decided to play on him a second time? He didn't think he had it in him to bear heartbreak once again.

His arms went rigid as he fisted his hands at his sides. Why on earth had Sadie brought Isaiah here?

"Levi."

The stern tone of Rachel's voice halted his dark thoughts.

"Whatever you are thinking, don't."

Sadie got out of the back seat. He watched as she tipped her head back, laughing at something her sister said. *Her sister.* Sara and

Isaiah were walking side by side with Sara's arm linked through his.

Not believing what he was seeing, he glanced at Rachel, who was looking very smug. "I don't understand."

Rachel gave him a pat on the arm. "I think it best if Sadie explains the situation to you."

He left the table and crossed the lawn, meeting Sadie halfway between the buggy and the picnic area. "I think we need to talk."

She nodded.

"Let's go around to the back of the house. On the way you can tell me about your sister and Isaiah."

"The short version is Sara has always been the Fischer *dochder* for Isaiah," Sadie said with a shrug. "I suspected her feelings for some time."

"And you didn't say anything sooner?"

"Because I needed to be sure. Look, Levi, you've known my *vader* had his mind set on a match between Isaiah and myself. I knew better."

"I see," he said, even though he didn't.

Sadie went on to explain. "Once we convinced our *vader* that Sara was meant for Isaiah, and Isaiah decided that Sara was indeed the better fit, he gave his blessing to them."

Levi still didn't understand how he hadn't seen any of this coming. "Interesting. And what about you? Has he given his blessing to you?"

Sadie stopped along the path. The look on her face told him everything. "I'm afraid not yet." She lifted her eyes to meet his.

Levi wanted to wipe away her doubt.

"He's not sure about you, Levi. But I am. I know there are things in your past—things you've kept from me. Perhaps it's time to let me in."

"Can you tell me what the school board said first?"

"All right. I have some news to share. Except I'm not sure if it's bad or *gut*. I've got the envelope here in my pocket. Someone gave it to my *vader* to give to me."

Stopping along the path, he looked down at her. He could almost read the doubt about her future in her eyes. Reaching down, he caught her hand. Her skin felt warm and soft beneath his calloused fingertips.

Giving her hand a reassuring squeeze, he said, "Remember what I said to you yesterday? How no matter what happens, you'll still have all of us to get you through?"

"I do remember." Sadie dropped his hand

and took the envelope out of her pocket. She nibbled on her lower lip.

Levi felt his heart lurch. If the news was not what she'd hoped for, she'd be upset. One thing he knew for certain was her strength would get her through.

She took a deep breath, then ran her finger under the flap of the envelope. Exhaling, she pulled out a note. "I'm almost too afraid to look."

"Do you want me to read it to you?"

"Nee."

Her gaze skimmed the page. And then her face broke out into the widest smile he'd ever seen.

"*Gut* news, I take it?"

"Yes! Yes! I'm staying. They want me to stay!"

Levi brought his arms around her, hugging her close, feeling her trembling with excitement. He let her go, saying, "Oh, Sadie, this is the best news for you."

"The only thing that would make it better is if you were going to tell me that you've decided to stay."

He'd decided more than that. "I have something I need to tell you."

* * *

Sadie wanted more than anything to hear Levi tell her that he loved her and that he would never leave her. She let him take her hand once more, relishing the warmth and security his touch brought her. She loved this man more than life itself. She wished this trepidation she felt every time they drew closer would leave. Only Levi could make the sensation go away.

"Does this something have to do with Jacob's offer?"

"*Ja*. And there's more." He led them to a bench under a big maple tree. "Come sit. I want to tell you about what brought me here."

She tilted her head to see him better. "I thought you came to help your cousin."

"That was part of the reason, but not all of it."

Sadie put a hand on either side of his face. Rubbing her thumbs along the hard plane of his cheekbones, she felt his strength. "Levi, in order for us to work, you need to tell me what is in your heart. I know you've been holding a pain deep inside. I saw it the first day I met you."

Sadie remembered how businesslike he'd been with her then, practically ordering her out of the wagon, and how mad he'd gotten when she didn't tell him right away where she lived. And the other times when he'd pushed her away…

But the day Robert King had come into her classroom, intent on making her at fault for Mica's learning problems, that day had been the turning point. Levi had been there for her, and now she wanted to be there for him.

"Tell me what happened to you."

Putting his hands around hers, he said, "This isn't easy for me. None of this has been easy for me." Touching his forehead to hers, his voice broke. "Falling in love with you should have come easily. And yet, I've tried to fight those feelings from the moment I set eyes on you."

"Why?"

"Because my heart had been broken." He shifted away from her, resting his hands on his knees. "This situation is difficult for me to talk about."

Sadie's heart began to race. What if she were forcing him to relive something too painful? "I'm so sorry."

"I've been in love before." He stopped and then started speaking again. "That's not right. I thought I'd been in love. I wasn't."

Sadie let the words sink in. There had been someone else before her.

"A young woman. A lot like you." He turned to look at her then. "Pretty and impetuous."

"I'm not—" She was about to say *pretty*, but Levi held up a hand, stopping her.

"Sadie, you asked me to tell you. Please, let me continue."

Folding her hands in her lap, she nodded.

"We fell in love quickly. Again, I thought at the time the feeling was love. I'd known Anne for a long time. We grew up in neighboring communities. I met her at a picnic. The time seemed right, and my family might have been pressuring me to find a wife. I know you understand."

"I do."

"To this day I'm not sure what thoughts were in Anne's head. I only know she left me a note, telling me she'd decided to leave the community."

"You mean she wanted to move?"

"*Nee*. She wanted to leave the Amish life."

Sadie gasped. She couldn't imagine walking away from the only life she'd ever known. The thought of being shunned brought tears to her eyes. The idea that she'd have to leave her family, friends and the *kinder* she taught to be all alone in the *Englisch* world? *Nee.* She couldn't fathom how someone would want to do that.

Swallowing a sob, Sadie, barely got out, "Why? Why would she want to leave?" Worse yet, why would she push a man as wonderful as Levi away?

He looked out over the yard, unable to meet Sadie's gaze. "She was in love with someone else. An *Englischer.*"

"Oh, Levi. I'm so very sorry."

"You must understand how hard this has been for me. I wanted to start a new life with her, and she had met another man and fallen in love. I can forgive her, because she never would have found happiness with me. But when it first happened, I was angry and hurt. I know now that Anne and I weren't meant to be together. But I can't forget how her actions made me feel."

"But, Levi, I'm not that woman." Sadie shook her head. "I would never treat you like that."

"I know."

"And the situation with Isaiah, well, that was my *vader*'s doing from the very beginning."

"I know that. Though I have to tell you I wasn't sure what to think when I saw him getting out of the buggy just now."

Sadie realized her mistake not telling him about Isaiah and Sara when she saw him yesterday. "I guess I should have told you about the change in plans."

"That would have been helpful."

He stood up, shoving his hands in his pockets. "I wasn't sure I'd ever be able to trust my heart to love anyone again. And then I met you, Sadie Fischer. You turned my world upside down and right side up."

Sadie's heart soared. But she had to be sure he understood, no matter what, that she wasn't like this other woman.

"Levi, I would never be like Anne who broke your heart."

"You can't deny you've had an idea of the kind of man you wanted to spend the rest of your life with. Not too old, not too young..." His voice drifted off.

She knew those words might come back to haunt her for the rest of their days together. Defending herself might not be an easy thing, but she had to at least try. "I've *never* thought of you as such. You are a kind and decent man. One who is *gut* with the *kinder*. One who delivers on his promises."

"As little as a week ago, I would have told you that none of those words matter," Levi said. "Then I heard Robert King raising his voice to you, and the only thing I could think was I needed to keep you safe."

"I told you the other day, I had the situation under control."

"I remember. But I knew then that if I left here, I might very well be leaving something *gut* behind. I've been fighting this feeling for too long." Splaying his hands wide, he said, his voice broken, "I didn't want to risk my heart again. Do you understand what I'm saying?"

This time the wrenching sob came from her. Standing, she almost couldn't bear to ask him, "Levi, then you don't deny there is something between us?"

"Oh *ja*, there is more than something between us. I've fallen in love with you, Sadie."

Sadie clung to his side. Looking up at him, she needed to know if they had a future.

"Does this mean you're staying? Before you tell me what you're about to do, let me tell you how much I love you. Levi, my world righted the day I met you. You weren't too old or too young or heaven forbid already spoken for."

Levi let out a laugh. "You're not going to let that go, are you?"

"Nope."

"I don't know why I thought I could ever leave you."

"Wait!" she said suddenly. "You need to tell me your other news."

"My other news?"

"*Ja*... Jacob's offer. Are you going to accept it?"

"I signed the papers this morning."

"*Ach!* That's wonderful!" Sadie fell into his arms. "I love you, Levi Byler."

"I love you, too, Sadie Fischer. More than life itself."

Tipping her chin up, he looked down into her eyes. Sadie's heart melted at the love she saw reflecting back at her.

Levi bent his head low. His mouth brushed against hers, his touch sending her heartbeat soaring.

"If you don't mind," he said quietly, "I want to give you a proper kiss."

She didn't mind at all. Standing on her tiptoes, Sadie met him halfway, their lips touching.

Lifting his lips from hers, he asked, "Can I tell you again how much I love you?"

"You can. Over and over and over." Sadie didn't think she'd ever been happier.

"I've finally found my home," he said with a smile.

"And I've finally found my perfect Amish man."

* * * * *

If you loved this story,
pick up Tracey Lyons's other book
A Love for Lizzie.

And be sure to check out
these other books set in Amish country:

The Baby Next Door *by Vannetta Chapman*
A Secret Amish Crush *by Marta Perry*
Amish Baby Lessons *by Patrice Lewis*

Available now from Love Inspired!

Sadie's Blue-Ribbon Snickerdoodle Cookies

1½ cups sugar
½ cup butter, softened
½ cup shortening
2 large eggs
2 ¾ cups all-purpose flour
2 teaspoons cream of tartar
1 teaspoon baking soda
¼ teaspoon salt
¼ cup sugar
2 teaspoons ground cinnamon

Heat oven to 400 degrees.

Mix the first 1½ cups sugar, the butter, shortening and eggs in a large bowl with hand mixer until light and fluffy. Stir in flour, cream of tartar, baking soda and salt until soft dough is formed.

Shape dough into 1¼-inch balls. Mix ¼ cup sugar and the cinnamon in a small bowl. Roll balls in the mixture. Place two inches apart on an ungreased cookie sheet.

Bake 8 to 10 minutes or until set. Remove from cookie sheet and cool on a wire rack.

Dear Reader,

I wrote this book during a difficult time in my life. My dad had just passed away. I remember writing the proposal for Sadie and Levi's story at the same time I was working on my dad's obituary.

My point is, we never know what life is going to bring us. But hopefully we find the happiness that lies just around the next corner.

The hero of this book had no intention of falling in love. He wanted to mend his broken heart and start fresh in a new town, while the heroine wanted nothing more than to find her perfect match. Sadie and Levi seemed to go head-to-head while repairing a damaged schoolhouse, but then found a way to work together. Circumstances brought them together and they both learned that they could set their differences aside to find true love and happiness.

I hope you enjoyed their story as much as I enjoyed writing it.

Special thanks to my editor, Melissa

Endlich, and my agent, Michelle Grajkowski, who always steer me in the right direction. As always, special thanks to my husband, TJ.

Happy reading!
Tracey

COMING NEXT MONTH FROM
Love Inspired

Available April 27, 2021

HIDING HER AMISH SECRET
The Amish of New Hope • by Carrie Lighte

Arleta Bontrager's convinced no Amish man will marry her after she got a tattoo while on *rumspringa*, so she needs money to get it removed. But taking a job caring for Noah Lehman's sick grandmother means risking losing her heart to a man who has his own secrets. Can they trust each other with the truth?

TO PROTECT HIS CHILDREN
Sundown Valley • by Linda Goodnight

Struggling to find a nanny for his triplets, rancher Wade Trudeau advertises for a housekeeper instead. So when former teacher Kyra Mason applies, looking for a place without children to recover after a tragedy, she's shocked to meet his toddlers. Might this reluctant nanny and heartbroken cowboy find healing together?

A PLAN FOR HER FUTURE
The Calhoun Cowboys • by Lois Richer

Raising his orphaned granddaughter alone seems impossible to Jack Prinz, but he has the perfect solution—a marriage of convenience with his childhood friend. But even as Grace Partridge falls for little Lizzie, convincing her to marry without love might not be so easy...

THE TEXAN'S TRUTH
Cowboys of Diamondback Ranch • by Jolene Navarro

Returning to his family ranch, Bridges Espinoza's surprised to find his cousin's widow—the woman he once secretly loved—there as well. But even more stunning is the boy who arrives claiming to be his son. While the child brings Bridges and Lilianna together, the truth about his parentage could tear them apart...

THE SHERIFF'S PROMISE
Thunder Ridge • by Renee Ryan

After Sheriff Wyatt Holcomb and veterinarian Remy Evans clash over her new petting zoo—and her runaway alpaca!—the two strike a bargain. She'll watch the nephew in his care for the summer if he'll push along the permit process. But keeping things strictly professional is harder than either of them expected.

SEEKING SANCTUARY
Widow's Peak Creek • by Susanne Dietze

When pregnant single mom Paige Latham arrives in Kellan Lambert's bookstore needing a temporary job, he wouldn't dare turn away the sister of his old military buddy. But as they grow closer working together, can they say goodbye before her baby arrives, as planned?

LOOK FOR THESE AND OTHER LOVE INSPIRED BOOKS WHEREVER BOOKS ARE SOLD, INCLUDING MOST BOOKSTORES, SUPERMARKETS, DISCOUNT STORES AND DRUGSTORES.

LICNM0421